THE ARCHITECT'S SUICIDE

THE ARCHITECT'S SUICIDE

a fictional account

R. M. BECKLEY

iUniverse LLC
Bloomington

THE ARCHITECT'S SUICIDE
A FICTIONAL ACCOUNT

Copyright © 2014 R. M. BECKLEY.

All rights reserved. No part of this book may be used or reproduced by any means, graphic, electronic, or mechanical, including photocopying, recording, taping or by any information storage retrieval system without the written permission of the publisher except in the case of brief quotations embodied in critical articles and reviews.

This is a work of fiction. All of the characters, names, incidents, organizations, and dialogue in this novel are either the products of the author's imagination or are used fictitiously.

About the Characters
Characters and institutions in the novel that are named and well known are used only for their ability to bring this novel to life, and there is no intent to represent them in any manner. The identities of others in this novel are fictitious, and any similarities to those living or dead are purely coincidental.

iUniverse books may be ordered through booksellers or by contacting:

iUniverse LLC
1663 Liberty Drive
Bloomington, IN 47403
www.iuniverse.com
1-800-Authors (1-800-288-4677)

Because of the dynamic nature of the Internet, any web addresses or links contained in this book may have changed since publication and may no longer be valid. The views expressed in this work are solely those of the author and do not necessarily reflect the views of the publisher, and the publisher hereby disclaims any responsibility for them.

Any people depicted in stock imagery provided by Thinkstock are models, and such images are being used for illustrative purposes only.
Certain stock imagery © Thinkstock.

ISBN: 978-1-4917-3444-5 (sc)
ISBN: 978-1-4917-3445-2 (hc)
ISBN: 978-1-4917-3446-9 (e)

Library of Congress Control Number: 2014908302

Printed in the United States of America.

iUniverse rev. date: 05/16/2014

TABLE OF CONTENTS

PROLOGUE

Robert A. Michael, architect, disappeared some time ago. So why am I writing about him now? Robert desperately wanted to join the pantheon of modern architectural heroes. The architectural profession that was conceived by architects in the first half of the twentieth century seems to have vanished along with Robert. His disappearance greatly disturbed me. The so-called modern era for architects and their profession appears to have come to an end.

I was asked by a publisher to select an architect whom I could write about as a contribution to an encyclopedic endeavor. As an architectural critic I have written about many living architects. The publisher's goal was to capture the zeitgeist of late twentieth-century architecture as we entered the twenty-first. Excited to be offered this opportunity, I could think of nothing more appropriate than selecting an architect who had recently gained renown by his disappearance.

Robert had the overinflated ego that architects of this period were known for. I believed Robert's tale was important to tell because it revealed the problematic nature of architectural practice during the latter part of the twentieth century, especially for someone with Robert's aesthetic ideals.

To begin this project I did what any journalist would do: I interviewed people who knew Robert. The following stories are derived from notes made during those interviews. Some liberties have been taken in editing these transcripts to give each interviewee the opportunity to describe their personal relation with Robert. I confess that, to make them more provocative reading, I especially chose interviews that captured Robert's idyllic nature. In so doing I hope to reveal the challenges he and his profession faced during his time. It may take another half century to understand what actually happened to Robert, his disappearance, and the profession he idolized since he was a teenager. A profession that he felt had betrayed him. Unfortunately, the publishers were unable to complete their own heroic ambition. I have decided to publish my edited interviews nonetheless.

Perhaps I have not captured the nuances of each narrator's voice. I am a journalist and not a poet. What is important is what each individual has revealed about the architect Robert A. Michael and his struggle to maintain his modern ideals at the same time nurturing a viable architectural practice during the latter half of the twentieth century. I hope these narratives might help explain his despondence, disappearance, and possible suicide, and meanwhile may they shed light on what happened to architectural practice during that period.

> *There will always be myths, whether they are handed down from antiquity or created by the media. And these myths will always sustain the possibility of heroes. Thus the question may not be whether it is still possible to be a hero, but whether it is possible to recognize a hero who eludes classification and thereby endures in spite of a culture of mediation.*
>
> —Cynthia C. Davidson, *Any* 1, no.2 (September/October 1993): 5

INTRODUCTION: THE AGE OF HEROES

The Critic

I have known Robert A. Michael better than most of the architects I have written about. He had his studio in Printer's Row, not far from my own office. I ran into him frequently. He practiced architecture. I wrote about it. We would share adjoining stools at our neighborhood bar. After Robert had a few gin martinis he had a tendency to bare his soul during both the best and worst of times. I recall how frequently he said he had once embraced the image of the architect created by Ayn Rand in her best-selling and controversial novel *The Fountainhead*. Thinking about Robert's disappearance and his possible suicide, I am reminded of the book's last passage, which Robert had memorized. Howard Roark, the heroic figure created by Rand, is pictured standing at the top of the city's tallest skyscraper, one of his design and still under construction. He is about to be met by his lover, who ascends to meet him in an open construction elevator. Robert had memorized the last passage in the book and enjoyed reciting it to me:

> The line of the ocean cut the sky. The ocean mounted as the city descended. She passed the pinnacles of bank buildings. She passed the crowns of courthouses. She rose above the spires of churches. Then there was only the ocean and the sky and the figure of Howard Roark.

Robert told me that he imagined Howard Roark looking out at the horizon, the place where ocean meets sky, from the pinnacle he had himself created. A fascination with the horizon would play a significant role in shaping Robert's aesthetic vision throughout his life, a vision no doubt inspired by this passage.

For many impressionable boys still in their youth and considering career options, *The Fountainhead* captured their imaginations despite their lack of understanding of Rand's libertarian philosophy of objectivism. It didn't hurt a young boy's imagination that the "she" in the passage above was none other than the former Dominique Wynand, Roark's lover, a model with a beautiful body and sophisticated air, "the perfect priestess" in her creator's own words. That book inspired many young men to pursue architecture as a profession even as they would later blame Howard Roark and Ayn Rand for falsifying what it meant to be an architect. The book is still read by Rand devotees. Robert, in a moment of candor, told me that even as a teenager who wanted to become an artist, he could imagine himself as Howard Roark.

Another marker in Robert's development as an architect occurred twenty-two years after the publication of *The Fountainhead.* One of the last modern heroes, this one not fictional, went for a swim in the Mediterranean Sea only to drown near his cabin in Roquebrune-Cap-Martin in southern France. Le Corbusier, the Swiss architect who adopted France as his home and changed his name from Charles-Edouard Jeanneret, spent his last years there, and it was there where his life ended. Was it an accidental or a suicidal drowning? Most biographers have given Corbu (a nickname used by his acolytes and others) the benefit of the doubt and attributed his death to a heart attack. Corbu's death had a profound effect on Robert, who in that same year, 1965, was opening a studio and launching his own career in architecture. Robert imagined Corbu swimming for the horizon, obviously an unobtainable goal, just as Roark stood atop his skyscraper still under construction, arms folded and feet apart, gazing at the horizon and defying death while the wind tried to dislodge him from his perch. Both these giants of imagination, one literary and the other manufactured by a superego, helped to establish the image of the architect as hero, the autonomous architect, an image that would become an important part of modernist lore and a goal, even in his later years, for Robert A. Michael, architect.

Robert's disappearance seems to have been well designed, an acknowledgment that Robert would appreciate coming from this critic. (Hello, Robert; are you reading this?) Everyone—clients, employees, friends, and family—agree that Robert would have the impulse to design his own death rather than leave it to chance.

In trying to understand Robert's supposed suicide, my research revealed that in the 1800s the French sociologist Emile Durkheim had argued that suicidal feelings occur as a response to a person's relationship to society, to not being a part of a community or to sudden disruptions in the fabric of daily life. Sigmund Freud later observed that suicide could be put in the same category as masochism, which he attributed to an aggressively critical superego turning on the self. I have heard Robert himself say, "Suicide is the ultimate ego trip." Freud would have agreed, it seems.

Robert was an ordinary guy. That is how he described himself to me, this architectural critic, even as he hoped I would disagree. Born of ordinary parents in an ordinary city in an ordinary house in the Midwest, he told me that he found drawing and math to be creative outlets for his imagination. But after reading *The Fountainhead* he decided that he wanted to be more than ordinary. He believed that he was a modern man, living in modern times, as he was tutored and inspired by the controversial author Ayn Rand. He had little regard for history. He aspired to the artistic and individualistic ideals of modernism. He believed in a world that could be created from new aesthetic sensibilities, new technologies, and new programs. Living near Chicago, he grew up in the shadow of many of America's early modern architects—heroes and innovators—Burnham and Root, Adler and Sullivan, Jenny, Frank Lloyd Wright, and others. But Robert thought it was the Bauhaus transplant Ludwig Mies van der Rohe, who moved from Germany to Chicago to direct the architecture program at the Armour Institute of Technology, who best epitomized modern ideals. It was Mies who was credited with the manifesto "less is more," a manifesto that Robert adopted as his own aesthetic credo.

To some, Robert's life might read like a soap opera. His accomplishments, I know, did not live up to his expectations. That is no aspersion of his talents. Robert wanted to live in the heroic era of modernism. Was he simply a man born into the wrong era? Ayn Rand's character Howard Roark was conceived in a time of heroics but read about in a time when heroism was beginning its decline. Now it is nearly impossible to imagine heroism to be a part of the contemporary practice of architecture. Corbu, Wright, dead—the great monuments of modern architecture had already been produced and confined to the history books by the time Robert began his practice. Henry Russell Hitchcock and Philip Johnson put nails in modernism's coffin with their 1930s exhibit at the Museum of Modern Art and the publication of their book, *The International Style,* which followed. They turned what should have been a testimony to the future of architecture into a brand.

Robert was not without significant accomplishments—in his time. The wall of the reception area that provided entrance to his studio attested to the many design awards he had received for built commissions and even un-built projects.

Robert's architectural practice, like most others, experienced economic booms and suffered through economic depressions. When his firm appeared to be going under, he would find ways of surviving, new ventures, new ways of doing business, new kinds of commissions, exercising creativity combined with strong survival instincts. Like an amoeba, his firm would expand and contract and break into pieces dependent upon the environment for practice at the time. Robert's passion was not creating a successful business or attacking the day's pressing social concerns. Having grown up in the Midwest, he was a pragmatist. He claimed that rationalists occupied the East Coast and empiricists occupied California but pragmatists occupied the Midwest. Architecture for Robert meant creating the kind of poetry that could only be realized through building. Despite the fact that many architects his age during difficult economic times when clients were scarce were amusing themselves by reading French philosophers and developing new theories of architectural design doing "paper architecture," Robert only wanted to build.

A failed first marriage, a dead son he had hoped would someday be a partner, a grown daughter whose house he designed and that played a starring role in her divorce, changes in his client base, church leaders more concerned with doing good deeds than building striking edifices, changes in the technologies used for designing and building, changing markets—these all contributed to his frustration. Finally there was the love affair and fateful relationship with a publicist who helped him land the opportunity of a lifetime, an opportunity that ultimately blew up in his face because of his poor judgment and naiveté.

Robert was critical of the world of criticism. Once he told me, "If words can kill, I will soon be dead. The only thing worse than the noise that critics make is their silence, and I have been killed by both their noise and their silence." Robert was right. Fame is something you must chase, a chase that can be futile and even self-defeating. Fame is created through public relations, professional networks, and the cultivation of recognition. The goal is to become "recognizable." To be famous one *must* be recognizable. It is common knowledge in the arts that even a bad review is better than no review at all. But the reviewers, journalists like myself, given even the best project, are obliged to create a spin that will cast the project in a light the reviewer believes will be publishable, a light that will titillate the reader and bring attention to the critic. So the critic brings the architectural project into the light and out of the dark. Perhaps some of that light will fall on the architect, if he or she is lucky or if the object in the light is easily recognized as being a part of the architect's aesthetic, his or her brand, a contribution to his or her fame.

Architectural projects, for the most part, are born in anonymity. Unless brought under a spotlight, they are not commented on; they might as well not exist outside their immediate neighborhood. If brought to the attention of critics, then what shall we say? If we say something nice, we will be criticized for not being thoughtful enough, pandering to the establishment of taste makers, selling out to commercial or particular aesthetic, building or development interests.

The critical world has its own star system. Most buildings outlast their author and the public soon forgets what critics have written, but the building will stay around to make its presence known . . . or not. For many architects, their first work is their best. As they build more, the newness of their aesthetic wears off. They are soon remembered for what they did, not for what they are doing. As critics we are obliged to look for the newest. The established can be overlooked, simply ignored, or reduced to a footnote.

It is pure speculation as to how soon the spotlight swings away from even the most celebrated architects in today's media-saturated world. Being in the Midwest where there are far fewer spotlights for architects than in the media capitals of the east and west, it is especially difficult to capture the spotlight for recognition unless, perhaps, once in the spotlight you unexpectedly disappear and the spotlight begins a search for you, as was the case for Robert A. Michael, the architect. I feel that these stories are a part of that search.

. . .

I do not recall how many people I interviewed for this project. Some were very cooperative, and others not. Nearly a year had passed since Robert's disappearance when I began my interviews. It was not difficult for people to refer to Robert in the past tense. You may not be interested in reading all the interviews. These are the ones that most interested me. They need not be read in any particular order, though there is something of a chronological coherence to them.

IN SEARCH OF FAME

Wife No. 1

The critic asked me if I would say something about Bob. My first reaction was no. It has been years since we parted company—years since we saw each other last. But I do know things about Bob. The critic insisted, hoping I might shed some light on Robert's disappearance and his past. (I almost forgot that he had turned his identity into that of Robert A. Michael.)

Robert had always been called Bob. But on his applications to graduate schools, of course he used Robert as his first name. Since he had no middle name, where the graduate application forms asked for one he simply put the letter A. His initials, quite by accident and without forethought, came to be RAM. These initials would hold ever-greater meaning for Robert as his career unfolded. Robert applied to graduate schools that were all located on the East Coast and protected by ivy. Once enrolled in graduate school, he thought Bob gave away his Midwest origins, and he began to use his given name Robert, the name everyone now knows him by.

I didn't know what an architect was. There were none in my family and none among my family's friends and acquaintances. When Robert said on one of our first dates that he wanted to become an architect, I registered no feeling at all. I had no knowledge of what his profession would mean to our lives. None whatsoever. As it turns out, Robert didn't have much of an idea either.

Robert and I were sweethearts. The classic Eisenhower era kind where it didn't make much difference what you wished for because everyone was wishing for the same thing, a spouse, a house, a car, and kids. I wished for Bob senior year in high school, and I followed him to college. Well before we were married, he became wedded to his studies. He wanted to be an architect. We dated. We made plans. We talked about marriage. Bob was going to go off to graduate school to continue his architectural studies. *But what about me, Bob?* There was no reason for him to take me with him to Harvard and its Graduate School of Design, the GSD. Unless, unless I got pregnant. Slam bang thank you, ma'am. I wore no diaphragm that one night and I knew. Yes, I knew. Remember that this was before the pill. The marriage was a hurried affair, just like the night I got pregnant. Nobody had planned this except me.

When Bob was in his teens, he expressed an interest in becoming an artist and began taking classes at the Art Institute. His parents decided that this was a big mistake, especially as his instructors kept encouraging him to do more with his obvious talent for drawing. It was Bob's father who encouraged him to use his artistic talent to become an architect, "a profession," he said, presuming that this "profession" could assure him a living income, frightened that Bob's talent would turn him into a starving artist. To seal the deal, Robert's father gave Robert the book *The Fountainhead* as a birthday present. *The Fountainhead* had been on the best-seller list getting mixed reviews, but Robert's father, even though he had not read the book himself, understood that it portrayed the architect in heroic fashion, just like the artists Robert most admired.

Mother was surprised when I announced the July wedding. It was already April. Father suspected something but didn't say anything. For Dad it was one fewer daughter to deal with, as he would announce inappropriately at the rehearsal dinner. Luckily I had two sisters who were married prior to me. The routine was down pat; Mom took over from there. Robert didn't care. His sight was focused on graduate school. He accepted that marriage was going to be an inconvenient interlude in his quest for fame. This was the first time I saw him get depressed. It seemed that this big move to graduate school with a wife in tow was something he hadn't bargained for.

"Let's get it over with and start our life," Robert declared. By now I was calling him Robert at his insistence. He thought first I had to get a job. "You've got a degree in library science, and Boston is full of libraries. No problem."

Nobody in my family did the math, counting the foreshortened period between marriage and the birth of Robert Jr. Free love was late coming to the Midwest, but it got there fortunately just in time for me, a nice middle-class white girl, to be forgiven for having developed an out-of-wedlock pregnancy. I thought Bob and I were in love; the classic "boy meets girl, boy and girl fall in love" kind of love, just as we were taught. It was pretty uncomplicated, except for Bob's quest for fame. That I believed would be a passing fancy once we had a family.

It wasn't our brains that attracted us to each other. Bob had hung out with an artsy crowd as an undergraduate before applying to graduate school. My best friends would be called nerds today. Opposites attract; maybe that was it. We had read some of the same books, including that damned book by Ayn Rand, *The Fountainhead.* He knew that I was not the Dominique Wyland that Rand created to be Howard Roark's lover and mistress. Bob loved that book, and I hated it. Bob imagined that he could emulate Howard Roark once he had his graduate degree.

Some people don't really get to know each other until after they are married. We developed our sexuality at the cusp of the sexual revolution. I was a little bit ahead of Bob in that regard, reading Simone de Beauvoir, Friedan, Steinman, and the whole feminist chorus. Men didn't have anything close to those dynamic publicists as references except Hugh Hefner, who warped men's expectations regarding the female body.

Opposites attract? But for how long? Eventually it gets old. It got old for us as careers, work, school, finances, kids, and Bob's ego and ambition all collided inside our marriage. Kids change everything, you know. And to have a kid just wiped out like Robert Jr. was . . . that kind of thing just changes your life. Bang. Life isn't the same anymore. And it never can be. There is the guilt. There is just too much of that to go around to be evenly distributed. It changed Bob's life. Mine too, of course. I guess I should say Robert now, because Robert Jr. was a product of Robert Sr. There was never a question of what a male son would be named. It was Robert's way of laying claim to this child conceived out of wedlock. *Wedlock*. What a strange word.

Robert was really a straight arrow. He felt very guilty that I got pregnant. I never told him that it was a plot on my part. And there was never a question that we would get married. That was just the way it was done. Even if we wanted an abortion, we would have no idea about how to proceed.

Graduate school was difficult for Robert. It seemed that the only way he could get through some days was to focus on an imaginary professional future. Robert Jr. and the way he learned fascinated him. He was convinced that he saw architectural talent in that little body. Perhaps he saw himself and was disappointed that he had taken so long to find his calling, even though the professors at the GSD made him question his own abilities day and night. It seemed sick when he started talking about Michael and Michael Architects. He was just putting too much stock in this kid, and the pressure would just grow to be something impossible, I thought. I couldn't imagine where this fantasizing of Robert's was going to go or how I could divert it. Robert was devastated when Robert Jr. was killed. His imaginary world shattered. I was afraid that he was going to drop out of school. He became morose. I can't say he became suicidal, but looking back that seems like a reasonable assumption.

I guess it was then that we made this silent pact. We'd get Robert through school, we'd conceive again and go about raising kids, and then . . . we were never able to talk about and then. Robert did graduate, not with honors as he had expected when he entered the GSD. Of course it was the professors' fault who didn't recognize his talents. To Robert he was at the top of the class. A genius.

Before graduation we did conceive again. Robert had a hard time accepting Amy, a petite little girl who held no resemblance to Robert Jr. and of course could never become an architect and her father's partner.

Robert wanted to stay on the East Coast after graduation. New York offered the best employment opportunities. He really wanted to work for Skidmore, Owings & Merrill. He had no trouble getting a job there with his Harvard degree in hand. Portfolios were what firms looked at, not grades. His portfolio clearly showed his reverence for Mies van der Rohe in his student designs. SOM had been founded in Chicago, and they too had been strongly influenced by Mies's minimalist aesthetic.

Life in New York became another kind of hell. No job for me. We lived in a hovel in the Village. All that life outside, but we had no money, one kid, Amy, and now another on the way. The breaking point for Robert came when a colleague, a fellow GSD grad, stole his drawings for a presentation. Robert nearly went berserk. If we owned a gun, I think there would have been some bodies lying around SOM. Robert's team had been working on a tight schedule and was getting ready for a client pin-up. They had worked late the night before but decided to all go home and get some sleep before the presentation. Robert was so beat, having stayed up until early morning for nearly a week, that he forgot to set the alarm clock when he got home, and he overslept. Of course he thought it was my fault that he had overslept, but I had no way of knowing that he was scheduled to participate in a presentation that morning. We talked little about his work. He took a cab uptown but was still fifteen minutes late for the meeting. All the drawings were pinned up, and here was his supposed colleague talking about Robert's drawings as though they were his own.

Robert never recovered from that. He learned something, I guess. But it launched a kind of paranoia toward his profession and others who practiced it. That was when he started putting his initials and date on every drawing he produced: RAM 00/00/0000. But his career at SOM was over as far as he was concerned. He said he'd never work for anyone else ever again. He vowed to start his own firm. His father, a realtor, offered him the opportunity to design some spec houses in his Chicago suburb. That offer also meant a ticket out of New York. No disappointment for me, but Robert's dream of making it in the east was finished. Robert was not sure about working so closely with his father. I told him that I thought it was worth a try. Our lives were miserable. He agreed. We packed.

Robert eventually found some space and started his office in downtown Chicago. To be honest, our life gets kind of fuzzy after that. I started working for an alternative bookstore, and those people became my "alternative family." The rest of the time I spent raising the kids, now two, Amy and Chip. Robert worked. I mean he worked. He was at his office (which he liked to call his studio) at least ten hours, most often twelve hours, a day. And when he wasn't there, he was out trying to make professional contacts and trying to get work. He joined the Young Founders Club at the museum and joined an avant-garde film society and was chosen for its board. He even joined the Chamber of Commerce so he could be part of their group insurance plan. He wanted me to participate in all this stuff, but I hated cocktail party chatter with people pretending to be who they weren't.

The place I was working had really neat people who held potluck suppers every other Friday night where everyone would bring their kids and pitch in and we'd talk about what we were reading, smoke some pot, and drink cheap wine. I got Robert to attend one night. That was an absolute low point in our marriage. We both went home stoned and started yelling at each other and cursing and throwing stuff. The house was a mess the next morning with the kids screaming in our ears. Without the help of New York, we had been able to create another little hell. We pretty much led separate lives after that. We still lived together. We would even have sex on occasion, but the love had gone out of our marriage. It was the sexual revolution. We could find uncomplicated sex outside of marriage. I think that's an oxymoron. We liked to think it was uncomplicated, but it never was. I don't know about now. At least by then we finally had the pill and didn't have AIDS to worry about yet.

Our marriage just fell apart. We were like two people on an ice floe that just imperceptibly breaks up as the water around it warms. Except that there were these two other little bodies on our breaking-up ice floe. Without discussing it, we had agreed to stay together until they were through school.

Another turning point in our relationship, and there were many, occurred when Robert's father gave us a piece of land. Abercrombie Heights had become a destination for many affluent upwardly mobiles who could afford property with fantastic views of Lake Michigan and the city. Robert had designed several spec houses for his father on property in the Heights. There was a property Robert's father thought was unbuildable, so he gave it to his son to see what he could do. Robert saw this as an opportunity, a huge opportunity, to build a house that could demonstrate his talents. He would be the client, the architect, and the builder. The problem was that we had no capital, only the property in our name. Robert imagined this to be an opportunity like the Case Study Houses were in California, which launched the careers of many West Coast architects. He begged me to approach my father for a loan. Robert's father had deeded title to the land to us, so we had some equity in the property. Dad, hoping to save our marriage, which was obviously on the rocks by this point, gave us a land contract. After persuading Dad to give us the loan, my task was over. Robert never consulted me on the design of the house. I don't think the idea ever crossed his mind. Robert's dream was built.

The house was really Robert's. I moved out when I couldn't take living in a Robert A. Michael and Associates, Architects, showcase any longer. It was never my home. It was like living in a furniture showroom, full of all this modern crap you couldn't sit on. I'd spend as much time as possible either at the bookstore or at friends' houses. If the kids and I weren't there, the house wouldn't get dirty or mussed up, and Robert wouldn't get annoyed that the house wasn't perfect when he'd unexpectedly bring a potential client home for a drink. We had this exercise down so well that we didn't even have to talk about it. Somehow I would know when I should be out of the house, and somehow he would know when I was. I guess in this sense we were closer together than ever in this kind of extrasensory kind of way—but further apart.

For Robert's graduation from Harvard I bought him a signed lithograph by Le Corbusier. He was Corb to everyone at the GSD, some of whom had worked for him in his Paris atelier, or so they said. The lithograph was signed "L-C 55. 1955 Le Corbusier Poeme de L'angle Droit Mourlot." Even then I had to borrow money from Dad for the purchase. After a little research Dad decided that the print might grow in value, so there was little back-and-forth over the nature of the bargain.

But since it was purchased with his money, he felt that it was as much his as it was Robert's, even though he cared little about its provenance.

The print shows an open hand, fingers apart and pointing upward. The hand might also be taken as the profile of a bird. It was an image that Corb painted frequently—the Monument of the Open Hand. From the prints I could have chosen there were also many of women, buxom women, bare-breasted women. Corb seemed to share Picasso's fascination with the female torso. That generation of artists pandered too much to Robert's taste, which still had a ways to grow, to mature. I settled on the open hand.

When it was presented at his low-key graduation brunch with his parents, Robert took the print from its tube and looked at it. He noted that Corb had signed the print L-C 55. I wouldn't appreciate that comment until after the SOM incident when Robert began to sign his own drawings RAM with a date. The print had meant something to him? I wasn't sure.

The print remained in its tube, just one of many similar cardboard tubes that Robert stored his own drawings in. It returned to Chicago with us, still coiled in the dark inner sanctum of its tube, protected from the light. It was only later, after we had separated when I visited Robert's office and saw it in a frame in his reception area, that I knew that he was having an affair with that bitch Medea from New York. He began to pay more attention to his trophies starting then. I doubt that he remembered that it was me who had given him that now highly regarded possession.

I knew that Robert had been having affairs with at least one of his clients and God knows who else. I didn't care. I was getting mine, though I envied the opportunities he had, all the excuses for late nights he had while I had to work my extramarital affairs around the kids' schedule. This women's liberation thing became a one-way street. Robert thought I was having an affair, and that liberated him to have an affair, and vice versa and etc., etc. The hand that opened the cage for us women was the same hand that caged us in the first place. It was still their cage, and we were still their pigeons.

Am I sorry Robert's gone? I'm sorry for the kids, Amy and Chip. They feel like they've played a part in his disappearance. But Robert? No. Maybe he is out there somewhere enjoying life's little pleasures. Or maybe not.

ATELIER, STUDIO, OFFICE

The Daughter

Why was the smell of Dad's office such a profound memory? Because, I suppose, I went there with him almost every Sunday morning. My younger brother, Chip, was invited to go along, but he knew that with Dad out of the house he could watch the Sunday morning cartoons on TV. Dad wasn't a religious man. Going to his office on Sunday morning I guess was a substitute ritual. I shouldn't say "office." Dad distinguished between his studio, an atelier, and an office. According to Dad, the studio was where a team of professionals made designs, an atelier was where things were made under the supervision of a master, and the office was where business was made. Some days his workplace would be a studio, others an atelier, and others an office. On Sunday mornings it was an atelier under the supervision of a master. He was the master, and I was the student. Once after stopping for some hot chocolate, a lure Dad used to get me to go with him, Dad would sit me down at his conference table with paper, pencil, and different colored magic markers to draw. He taught me how to draw plans, then elevations, then sections, then axonometrics, and finally perspectives. I asked more than once, "Will this make me an architect?"

More than once he answered, "No. Girls become interior designers, not architects. You will be an interior designer. Not an interior decorator. Interior designers can draw. You will become an interior designer because you can draw."

While I was busy drawing, Dad would work his way through the studio looking at drawings and models that were on each desk and occasionally making his own drawings to leave behind for someone to find when they came to work on Monday. Studio or atelier? It kind of depended on what role Dad wanted to play that day.

True, my most vivid childhood memory of that place was the smell of ammonia. Not the kind of ammonia smell that stinks up high school chemistry labs. No, this was the ammonia stink of wet diapers. Thirty years ago the smell of ammonia in an architect's office was the smell of success. It was the smell of prints being made, plans being duplicated. Blueprints had gone the way of wooden pencils. Each office could make its own prints using the diazo process, and small offices used this stinking process to reproduce prints with the exception of the voluminous drawings and written specifications that constituted construction documents. In the diazo machine, drawings on transparent paper were pressed against a glass plate with a lamp on the opposite side backed with a photosensitive paper. This weird greenish-tinted paper was bleached by the light and then subjected to a batch of ammonia fumes. The ammonia vapors passing over the paper once it was rolled in a metal tube transferred the image from the original to this sensitized paper.

One Sunday morning, when Dad noticed I had become extremely bored with drawing and he was taking too much time in the studio, he said, "Let me show you something," and he took me by the hand and up a very dark stair to the roof of his building. As we stood on the tarry substance of the roof, he said, "Look there," pointing at the building across the street, I thought. Then he lifted me on his shoulder and said again, "Look there." He was pointing beyond the neighboring buildings to the horizon where the sky met the lake and the two seemed inseparable. The beauty he saw in that vision seemed to be the sum of all of Dad's aesthetic aspirations where space and time seemed at one. Every Sunday morning if the weather was agreeable we would repeat that journey.

The smell of ammonia in the office came not only from the fresh ammonia bath but also from the paper itself, stacks of paper all over the office, paper that had been anointed in ammonia that had produced an image where light had been blocked by graphite or ink. Amazing that all these years later I still associate Dad's office with that smell, even long after his staff stopped developing prints using that method.

When I was older, Dad told me he looked for office space he could afford in downtown Chicago—something with character. Through friends he found someone looking for a partner to rehab a loft building in Printer's Row south of the Loop. Printer's Row, formerly the heart of Chicago's printing businesses, was a place some ambitiously thought might become Chicago's SoHo. Brick loft buildings with high ceilings, large unobstructed floor plates, and perhaps a working elevator dominated its few blocks, giving it that scruffy character with promise that especially appealed to artists, architects, and designers.

After Dad disappeared, the office had to be closed. His employees mostly found work elsewhere. It didn't take long for the office to show signs of inactivity while his partners in this real estate venture decided what to do. Until Dad could be declared dead rather than missing, their hands were tied. The white Helvetica letters that spelled out the name Robert A. Michael and Associates, Architects, on the glossy black door that led up the steep flight of stairs to his office still seemed to hang on for dear life. But the office had lost the semblance of organization that it once had. Stacks of books and yellowing magazines covered the Eames potato chip chairs that sat against a scuffed white wall. Their chrome base was peeling. The lacquer on the plywood seats was faded and worn off in spots. Some of the top laminate was chipped away at the corners. Had all this decrepitude occurred in such a short time, or had we just not noticed when there was activity in the studio of Robert A. Michael?

The reception area had not seen a receptionist in a while. Ms. Jones, the multitalented receptionist, office manager, and Jill-of-all-trades, had left to work at an upscale design/build office. The white laminate desk she had occupied stood like a sentinel guarding the working part of the office from intruders. Intruders, as Dad would refer to them, were for the most part tradesmen marketing a new this or that. On my occasional visits I had seen more than one ushered into the conference room adjacent to the reception area while Ms. Jones would decide if they had something worthy to offer and who in the studio might be disturbed to speak with them—if they passed that test. If unlucky, the huckster would be asked to leave a brochure or sample and departed with the hope that some knowledgeable person would retrieve it. Few would realize that Ms. Jones through her long tenure with Robert A. Michael knew what might or might not be of value to the firm. The bright red Knoll chair that remained behind the reception desk had once cradled Ms. Jones comfortably, but not so comfortably that she couldn't spring into action, when needed, at a moment's notice. The chrome Luxo lamp on the desk was now covered with dust.

The conference room table still held drawings, some in rolls, some laid flat, some folded over to briefcase size. Waiting. Waiting for whom? Waiting for what? Who did they belong to now? Nearly a year had passed since I last stepped into Dad's studio.

The wall opposite the reception desk was covered with framed documents and plaques. The frames were all black, every one alike. The mats for various awards, certificates, licenses, and diplomas had all started out their life as bright white. But now each was showing its age, and variations of their color became noticeable. The ink signatures on some of the certificates had begun to fade. The awards and certificates dated to the 1960s. Robert had every distinction he'd ever won or achieved framed and then mounted on this wall. The frames appeared to grow in number as the decades progressed, but it was hard to tell since the chronological display of the awards had given way to a visual order of expedient locations as the growing number of awards began to overwhelm the wall. I found one dated well before Dad disappeared. It was an honorable mention for a residence published in *House and Garden,* now *H&G*. Recognition had been given to the Smith House, which was called the Amy and Andy House on Robert A. Michael and Associates, Architects, construction documents prepared for me and my husband. Andrew and I insisted that our house be called the Smith House in any publication where it might appear, and it was, thanks to Medea's efforts. Dad knew that Andrew hated to be called Andy, and it remained a sore spot in Andrew's relationship with Robert throughout our marriage. The house was sold as part of our divorce agreement.

Andrew and I had asked Dad to design our house shortly after we were married. Dad's office was slow then. Without work was more like it. The recession had hit him hard. The only work he "had on the boards" were a few remodeling's, and he was nursing a church project, trying to convince his client that they could build a sanctuary that wouldn't go over their budget.

Dad complained about how unappreciative his clients were as we began to talk about commissioning him for our own house. He reminded us that it wasn't like the old days when someone would see one of his houses and come knocking on the door with a wish for a "Michael" house, bringing along a few magazine articles that talked of the "house of tomorrow." Now people came to him with a subdivision plan and pictures of the house they wanted to fit to their lot with this or that modification. No one was interested in the future anymore, he would often repeat. Everyone wanted a house that reminded him or her of the past. Something "cozy." And beside these clients he called Philistines, there were the bank loan officers who scoffed at anything that "looked modern."

Dad had become bitter. Bitter with his lot, bitter with his life, bitter with his clients, bitter with his bank, bitter with his wife. But he loved me. I could do no wrong. The evening Andrew and I invited him out for dinner at his favorite restaurant and announced that we wanted him to design a house for us because we were planning a family, his eyes lit up and all his bitterness seemed to disappear.

I was the middle child, one of three. A car in Cambridge killed Mom and Dad's firstborn, my older brother, Robert Jr., whom I never got to know. Dad was still in graduate school when it happened. They lived above one of the stores on Mass Avenue. Mom was working in a bookstore just up the street from their apartment. Some days, when he was around, Dad would take us to get Mom after picking us up from the babysitter. I was an infant in the stroller, and Robert Jr. would walk along side holding on, his legs steadied by the stroller that Robert Sr. would push slowly. The bookstore was just two blocks away. Robert Jr. seemed proud that he could walk, Dad said, if a one-and-a-half-year-old can express pride. That day, as Robert came to the corner, Mom saw us coming I was told and came out of the bookstore across the street to greet us. Robert Sr. didn't notice Robert Jr. release his grip on the stroller and step off the curb in the direction of his mother. He saw only the horrified look of the woman behind the wheel who brought her car to a screeching halt as she rounded the corner. But too late. Robert Jr. lay dead. A little life gone.

Dad and Mom were devastated. They each blamed themselves for the accident. The driver blamed herself. The whole incident took only a few seconds, but it changed the lives of three people, and one life was ended before it had hardly begun. I would ask my parents about my older brother, Robert Jr., and how he had died until I was old enough to realize how painful this memory was for them.

The doctor had encouraged Mom and Dad to have another child. Later they would tell me that they worried that it would be a boy or that it wouldn't be a boy. Robert Jr. couldn't be replaced, but somehow having a boy child might take away some of the sting. It was obvious that this child, were it a boy, could not be named Robert Jr. Robert Sr.'s dream of having a firm named Michael and Michael Architects ended with Robert Jr.'s death.

I could never have replaced Robert Jr. Mom and Dad never showed their displeasure with a girl once Robert Jr. was gone. But when I expressed a desire to become an architect in my early teens, Dad discouraged me, saying that architecture was not a field for women. I was enrolled in art classes and eventually attended the Art Institute, majoring in interior design.

It was actually Andrew's idea to commission Dad to design our house. He had received a promotion at the law firm; he was in line to become a partner, and his future looked bright. We picked out a lot. Andrew had already contacted a bank for a loan. Everything was coming together. And we both knew that Dad needed work.

Still, we had trepidations about hiring Dad to do our design. Robert had strong ideas. We knew that it would be more his house than ours. *How will we fare as clients?* we wondered. But this wasn't necessarily the house we would have all our life. Andrew had ambitions. His corporate clients liked his work. Other firms had approached him to go into partnership with them. So if this didn't work out, we could always sell the house and buy another. Would Robert understand if we didn't like what he designed? No. No way. If we bought a builder's house, Robert would be distraught. He would harangue us about what a terrible mistake we had made. He would critique the house's lack of a concept, its poor relation to the site, its poor quality of construction, its utter banality. No, there was only one way to avoid this. Dad, Robert A. Michael, architect, had to design our house.

"Hello," I said. I felt compelled to say hello. I was the little girl visiting my father's office once again hoping to find my father there. I remembered when I was only as high as the pencil sharpener that still hung on the wall and my eyes just came to the top of the reception desk. The reception desk was always clean and bright white. You could see Ms. Jones's reflection in it. She was always there, always with a friendly hello, asking me if I wanted to draw and providing me with magic markers and a clean sheaf of papers. I always felt at home there thanks in no small part to Ms. Jones.

Dressed in a black or white sheath dress in heels that brought her height to six feet and with a perfectly proportioned body, she moved like she might have been a dancer; she *had* been a dancer. She ran the office in style. Her blonde hair never aged, but the creases in her face reproduced with time. First crow's feet, or laugh lines around the eyes. Then the line around her mouth became more distinct. Her eyelids began to droop. She compensated with more makeup. And as the eyeliner got thicker, the mascara more colorful, and her lips turned to scarlet, her white and black dresses became foils for an always more colorful woman. The "kids," the name given to interns by Ms. Jones, who often were the largest population in the studio, had an influence on Ms. Jones. She was one of them in spirit. Introducing them to the lore of architectural practice, she would tell tales across a stool at the local bar or the coffee shop downstairs. It was the kids who fueled her perpetual youth. It was the kids who insisted that she put a red streak in her hair after they had seen a photo of her with just such a streak of crimson taken as she was about to receive her MFA from Yale.

But Ms. Jones was gone. We'd lost touch. She couldn't afford not to be paid. We found out that Dad owed her eight months' pay when she finally left. There wasn't much for her to do anymore. No money was coming in or going out, though people called wanting to be paid: the office supplies shop, the printers, and the insurance company. All the accounts were balanced. She had gone to the bank for Dad, pleading for an extension to the firm's line of credit. They were sympathetic, but there were no contracts to back up these extensions. Dad couldn't understand the bank's refusal to extend his line of credit. He had banked with First Trust for thirty years. Ms. Jones tried to explain that the management had changed after the bank's merger and none of the people he had dealt with for years were at the bank any longer. Dad couldn't deal with the changes and the humiliation of dealing with new bank people all the time trying to explain the shortcomings of his practice. He had handed over the banking to Ms. Jones. She was the one who now had to worry about the bottom line. It was she who was writing Dad his monthly draw even as she wasn't paying herself. It wasn't until she quit that Dad discovered that he owed her eight months in back pay. He was sick. Sick for not paying attention. Had she done him a favor by not telling him? He didn't know.

My "hello" hung in the air, held aloft by a cloud of memories and the faint smell of ammonia that simply never left the office of Robert A. Michael and Associates, Architects. It could also have been the sun's rays coming through the blinds filtered by the dirty windows that made the room seem hazy. I entered the studio, filled with this dirty light from the windows that overlooked the street below. My dad's office was at one end, and twelve desks lined the wall along the windows. My hello had traveled from the reception area into this room, and like the ammonia smell of yore seemed to hang there waiting. But there were no ears to hear my hello. "Hello" simply hung there filling the acoustical void just as light passing through the windows tried to fill the spectral void. "Hello, hello, hello" could be echoed a thousand times without a response.

I could remember most of the names of the people who had occupied those desks. They were extended family. Even though people came and went, once they were a part of Father's firm, they were always welcome around the table even after they left to take a job with the competition or opened a firm of their own. Dad harbored no resentment. He was proud he had given so many young people a start. Perhaps "self-satisfied" would be a better term. He felt he was giving these young souls something the academy had never given him: survival skills. The Michael School of Graduate Studies was a name he sometimes conferred to his office. He was the headmaster, teaching design and philosophy. Dad's right-hand man, Ray, taught how to put buildings together and how to talk with contractors. Ms. Jones taught how to run an office and eventually how to deal with creditors and banks. After a year in Dad's firm, anyone could start their own office, though most stayed longer, often moonlighting to help make ends meet as they tried to pay off student loans, buy a car, or start a family.

Robert hosted a seminar in his office to help architectural acolytes study for the difficult, nearly weeklong NCARB architectural exam. The National Council of Architectural Registration Boards conducted a test that was accepted by most of the states and even had international stature. Passing was a license that helped architects with their mobility. Sometimes before establishing themselves, architects found it necessary to follow the regional economic fortunes, which didn't necessarily shift in unison. Before the exam the studio was used as a study hall with kids from other offices coming in at night to cram with Dad's prodigy, using the office library, copy machine, and whiteboard. The office/studio became an atelier with Dad as the master.

Dad knew them all. If they passed or if they didn't, they were all invited to Dad's house after the exam results were announced. And win or lose, everyone got drunk. The exams were a necessary evil, necessary to make the profession a proper club. Anyone could pass who knew how to study, but one didn't always know what to study for, so taking the test was something of a crapshoot. If you passed, you were lucky. If you didn't, you were unlucky. There were few who didn't pass by their third try. Most passed on their second if they missed the first time. Failing gave you the clues you needed to have to pass the second time.

Failing the design part of the exam was an important rite of passage, because the judges were idiots and didn't know anything about design, Dad would say. If you passed design the first time, you had obviously copped out and had produced shit; Dad would tell those who had done no better in design than he had the first time. Then to verify what the real judges of architectural talent thought of his designs, he would refer to the design awards hung framed on the wall of the reception area. They still hang there. I was sure that if Dad had let me go to architecture school, I could have passed the exam on the first try.

FIRMNESS, COMMODITY, DELIGHT

The Architect's Observer

I stopped out of architecture school after my third year to work on the construction of a church sanctuary designed by Robert A. Michael and Associates. Construction jobs are hard to come by if you don't have a union card or an uncle in a trade who could be your advocate with his boss. With a few years of college under my belt, I could read drawings, and I was lucky to find a job as assistant to a construction supervisor. To get the job I had to promise to see the project through to completion before returning to school. The job paid well and gave me a chance to pay off some of my college debt, debt that seemed to be piling up faster than I could imagine ever paying off. Besides, construction gave me greater opportunity to see my girlfriend, impossible if I returned to school and its demands on my time. I didn't really like the design and theory courses they made you take in the fourth year, courses that had a reputation for being "mental." It was all so much academic bullshit to me. The juried reviews by pompous critics were worst of all. I really did need to get away from this academic babble and get my head together.

I soon met Robert, the architect, on one of his site visits. I told him that I liked his church design, and he seemed to like the fact that I was an architectural student getting some on-the-job training in construction. He also liked my asking him questions about the design. His answers always seemed to turn into a lecture on this or that—how Corbu or Mies had inspired him, had I read *The Fountainhead*, how much he had hated graduate school, why he didn't like Wright. Another favorite topic was how difficult it was to be an architect in a society consumed by consumerism . . . decision makers without a drop of aesthetic sensibility in their DNA, etc. Robert was a very embittered man. I hoped none of this would rub off on me. I loved my job.

My job as assistant to the supervisor was coming to an end in February with the completion of the church sanctuary, a magnificent structure whose simplicity and play with light I only appreciated after it was completed. It was too late to get back into school that term. I asked Robert if I could work for him until September when I planned to return to school and work toward my degree. Robert had another church project that was about to enter the construction documents phase and he could use another hand, and since I had already helped build one of his churches and was familiar with some of the details he used I would fit in right away. I was hired.

This would be my first job in an architect's office. I realized the advantage I had looking at working drawings from Robert's office and translating them into actual construction. Robert would describe his office as a postgraduate school, and it was, especially for those who didn't have the advantage I had in doing actual construction work. Those just coming out of school had to learn about architecture from a totally different perspective. September came and went, and I decided to stay out of school another year. I really enjoyed working on these construction documents and thinking about how a building was put together rather than dealing with the academic environment that stood between me and a degree.

Then what I thought was a blessing became a curse. Robert entrusted me to develop the construction drawings and then with observing the construction of the Amy and Andy House. To avoid confusion it should be noted that after the house was completed and had been published for its award-winning design it became the Smith House. Medea saw to that.

After a few discussions with Robert, his daughter Amy had the feeling that hiring Robert to design a house for Andrew and her might lead to disaster. It did. But it wasn't the kind of disaster she had imagined. Despite the objections of his daughter and son-in-law, Robert called the house-to-be the Amy and Andy House and that was the name that prominently appeared on the construction drawing title blocks. Andrew hated being called Andy, and Robert was the only person with the gall to call him that. Amy had told everyone in the office to call her husband Andrew, and she had told her dad too, but of course her word carried no weight with Robert. If Robert found something irritable to people, he loved to rub it in, to make it worse. So it was with the nickname he used for Andrew.

The construction documents were largely based on the exquisite model that KoKo, the newest hire, had made from Robert's sketches. KoKo did a masterful job of interpreting Robert's sketchy ideas drawn on tracing paper that left much to the imagination, but Robert's houses were pretty easy to figure out. Their minimalist aesthetic relied on basic construction technologies. But the house for Amy and Andrew was a greater challenge. Robert usually did the engineering on his residential work that wasn't much more challenging than looking through the construction manuals and using a little common sense. But this house had many challenges. First of all was the site itself, which was perched on a steep ravine overlooking a creek that led to the lake. The footings for the house had to be placed on piles, retaining walls had to hold up the driveway and swimming pool, and support of the extreme cantilevers of both the roof and exterior deck needed special consideration. Besides defying the forces of gravity, the structural engineering had to be concerned with updrafts carried by winds coming off the lake and funneled upward by the valley below. They could create powerful vertical forces capable of lifting the house off its foundations. Those same winds could create a negative pressure on the outside of the house, especially during the heating and cooling season when the house was closed and pressurized, causing exterior walls to want to blow outward similar to the forces caused by weather from tornadoes and hurricanes. But most problematic were the exaggerated cantilevers Robert insisted upon. His aesthetic reasoning was to create the strong horizontal so important to his idiosyncratic design, especially where there was a horizon to use as a reference. As the ravine widened approaching the lake, it beautifully framed the horizon where water met sky as seen from the vantage point of the site Amy and Andrew had chosen. When his engineer, Inham Rah, suggested shortening the cantilever, Robert knew aesthetic reasoning would only fuel an argument, so he invoked the argument that the cantilever provided necessary summer shading of the all-glass façade. Inham bought that argument.

After visiting the site with Inham, Robert and he agreed that the house should be constructed of lightweight steel members. Robert had already lost that battle once with Amy and Andrew, who insisted that the house be made with wood since they knew that Robert could be relied upon to insist that the structure of the house be exposed. They thought that Robert's own steel frame house was cold. Robert, using his personal form of very irritating irony, told them, "Nobody is going to care if your house was wood or steel when it is a pile of rubble on the valley floor." That didn't resolve the dispute, and Robert finally caved after meeting with Inham to see if they might achieve the cantilevers he wanted using wood. The matter was solved, we thought, when Inham proposed using a flitch plate for the cantilevers, a piece of steel sandwiched between two wood beams for added strength—a decision that would haunt the project later.

Battles between Robert and daughter and son-in-law raged through the schematic design phase. Even though the conference room door was closed for these meetings, the high-pitched voices of Robert and Andrew could be heard throughout the office. This went on through design development and preparation of the construction documents. Robert knew that Amy and Andrew would be at the site all the time inspecting what was going on. Robert did not want to contend with their whims on the site, especially in front of the construction workers. And even though on residential projects he did most site observation himself, he told me that I would be the one doing site observation of the Amy and Andy House. I was delighted, to have the opportunity to get out of the office into the real world of construction again. But I was concerned about my ability to play a role as Robert's surrogate and buffer to his clients, who were, after all, members of his family.

The first problem during construction occurred after the foundations had been poured and the framing begun. Eric, the construction foreman for the general contractor, informed me that the steel supplier was a whole month behind schedule on his deliveries. That meant that the steel flitch plates that were to form part of the cantilevered beams wouldn't be available for another thirty days, throwing the whole project off schedule. The general contractor had signed a contract with a move-in clause that guaranteed occupancy by December 1 so that Andrew and Amy could host the law firm's Christmas/Hanukah party. The contractor stood to lose a bundle of money if the project wasn't completed on time, even though it would be through no fault of his own. Andrew had his firm's contracts division look over the construction contract, and they added amendments that closed any loopholes there might have been in the standard construction contract. In exchange, the contractor got the contingency budget raised from 10 to 15 percent in consideration of the difficult site. Since the steel delivery was out of their control, the general contractor hoped the move-in clause would be null and void, like an act of God. In any case there was no way he could make up thirty days in the six months that were left, and he only hoped they would be able to get all of their equipment off the site before guests arrived for the party. Eric asked me what I wanted to do.

I asked back, "What are the options?"

"Forget the damn flitch plates," he replied. "They are like putting suspenders on a man wearing a belt. We do cantilevers like this all the time, without steel."

I didn't believe him, but I wasn't prepared to pretend to know enough to challenge him either. "Give me some more options," I said.

"Instead of steel, we can use plywood for the flitch plates. All the steel does is add stiffness to the wood members. Plywood will do the same thing."

"Let me talk with Robert," I replied.

I didn't intend to talk with Robert, but I wanted my response to carry some weight when I returned to the construction site. If I mentioned this to Robert he would go ballistic. His first response would be "Why did you let this happen?" addressed to me as though it were a problem I had created. Then he would probably say, "You can't do this to Amy and Andy. They are counting on this house being completed December 1. Andy's job is on the line, and so is yours."

Anyone who's ever worked with building construction knows how difficult it is to keep projects on time and within budget, even when a completion clause is at risk. But timing was one of the issues Robert and Andrew had wrestled back and forth with. Amy had stayed out of it. Andrew was determined to host the holiday party for the firm. It was his and Amy's coming out party. He had said as much. His time to step forward and show that he deserved the respect of the other associates and was partner material.

I went back to the site somewhat pissed. Why was I in the middle of this? "Just get the job done," I told Eric. The beams were up the next day. The job proceeded quickly after that. It was a shot of adrenaline for the contractor, as any athlete knows who has gone into the final quarter of a football game realizing that the team has a chance to win the game even though they are behind.

The crew was professional. They had worked on Robert A. Michael houses before. Robert had done the difficult work of establishing his standards of quality with the workers, whom Robert elevated to the status of craftsmen. Robert taught them to take pride in their work, even in such things as concrete formwork and plumbing fittings that no one would ever see. I enjoyed the fact they would call me over to see their work if I seemed not to be "observant" enough.

Robert was right. Amy and Andrew were at the site all the time, Amy less frequently. But sometimes I would be there at the crack of dawn because of a concrete pour or something critical going on and there would be Andrew in his suit and tie and wingtips, climbing over the concrete forms, gazing about. I never knew what he was looking for. I joked with him that the concrete crew was not part of the Mafia and he needn't worry about any bodies being laid in his foundations. He joked back, "That might be one way of saving some money." We had established a comfortable relationship, though I wouldn't call it warm. I was, after all, Robert's surrogate. I sensed that Andrew kept waiting for something to be screwed up.

After settling the problem of the beams, the construction of the house went seamlessly for the most part. It was difficult getting the pile driver down the hill and around the elm tree that Amy insisted on saving. The tree's roots and crown extended far into the site. The contractor said he could get the pile driver down the slope but he wasn't sure he could get it out. Within earshot of Amy and with a sarcastic tone to his voice, he asked me if I thought we could incorporate the pile driver into the design of the house. I could tell that this didn't amuse Amy. The pile driver was gotten out, though it cost the elm tree a huge branch that was intended to serve as an umbrella adding protection from the sun for the bedroom wing to the west of the house. Amy was further distraught when she saw the damage. "Well, ma'am, you've got the rest of the tree intact, and if it wasn't for us risking our necks out on that ledge you wouldn't have no damn house on this site." I remember the shocked expression on Amy's face. She wasn't used to hearing the mocking comments so often made by contractors who didn't appreciate their work being questioned. Though she had been to the site many times, she began at that moment to realize the effort it took to get the pile driver down the slope and the care the contractor had to take with anchoring it so that each blow into the hillside would not threaten the heavy machinery with a slide down to the valley floor below. She seemed just then to appreciate the risk the contractor was taking to build the Amy and Andy House on this particular site—risk not only to the machinery but also to the flesh and blood of those who operated it.

The move in was successful. The construction equipment was gone, the sod laid down, and the house made presentable, though Robert thought the furniture they had bought without consulting him was all wrong, disastrously wrong. The landscape would be redone once spring came, but for now people wouldn't get muddy arriving at the entrance. It was the way I imagined a movie set to be, with everything looking real but not quite real. One morning I arrived early as usual to make sure the masons were going to complete the brick driveway in the herringbone pattern we had specified. Andrew was there and said, "Hey, isn't your part of the job over? The caterer is coming tomorrow to inspect the kitchen for the party. It's not Robert A. Michael's house any longer. It is ours. See ya, pal." That was my last visit to the site and my last stint as Robert's surrogate.

The rest I've heard from Robert and the contractor and office gossip and read about in the newspaper. No one blamed me for what happened. I was grateful for that, but I still didn't sleep well at night. You see, the deck collapsed during the big holiday party. Thirty people were injured, two seriously. Amy and Andrew had hired a DJ to provide entertainment, and there was dancing of course. Because it became warm inside the house due to the body heat generated by dancing couples, some guests moved out to the deck and continued to dance. I couldn't even imagine thirty dancing people being able to fit on the deck. But they did, and before the party was expected to end the deck gave way. The insurance investigators spent weeks trying to figure out what went wrong along with sheriff deputies, who quickly determined that nothing criminal had happened. It appeared that the deck had buckled and pulled away from the house. The beams, minus their steel flitch plates, were also the cause of suspicion. Two of the beams were broken, but it was difficult to tell if they broke when they hit the retaining wall below or had already broken before they fell.

Andrew sued Robert and the contractor immediately, representing he and Amy, even though Amy, as one might expect, protested. I wondered whether it was ethical or even legal for Andrew to file a lawsuit representing himself. Andrew refused to talk with Robert or anyone else involved in the project. Another lawyer from Andrew's firm also sued, representing the injured. It was a mess. It went to trial. Witnesses were called. Some said they heard a crack before the deck crumbled, but others discounted the sound as part of the music. There were many contradictions in the testimony. The contractor refused to testify on his own behalf and was not subpoenaed by Andrew. Instead a lawyer and representative from the insurance company represented him. Robert had his own lawyer. Shortly after the trial began, the lawyers and insurance companies got together and settled. The trial was dismissed. The two who were seriously injured both recovered. One had to have his pancreas removed. The other still has some memory loss.

Robert told me that it was one of the darkest days of his career. He took the blame for putting someone with my lack of experience on the job, trying to take some of the blame himself but making me feel like shit. He was pissed that I hadn't consulted him about the flitch plate. But he was quick to turn the blame to Andrew. I remember him saying; "Those idiot kids should take their goddamn dancing to some goddamn nightclub where they could goddamn dance until the goddamn place fell apart. The DJ thing was Andy's idea, not Amy's. She just had to go along with her idiot husband's idea of a party." Over a beer after completion of the house, Robert expressed remorse that he had chosen to be an architect rather than an artist. "Some days the pleasure is simply not worth the pain." Those words still ring in my ear.

Robert believed in the strength of his intuitive skills. He always thought that your first idea was invariably the right one. He blamed himself for letting Andrew talk him into wood rather than steel construction. He told me that when he was beginning a design 90 percent of the time he would go back to his original idea after exploring alternatives. Intuition! Intuition informed by experience.

Robert taught me about the integrity of the construction process. There was little doubt that steel construction for the Amy and Andy House on that site would have been a better decision, aesthetics aside.

Even though Robert's moralizing was sometimes grating, once you looked past his holier-than-thou persona he was often correct. Robert hated to use wood in his houses or any building. "We've cut down too many trees." he'd say. "My father was guiltier than any. Everything had to be out of wood. The more wood, the better. Everybody likes wood. It's warm." He would quote his father as saying, "The more exotic the wood, the more they like it. Teak from Africa, redwood from California, and all those exotic hardwoods from the Amazon rainforest." Robert would say whenever we did use wood that we had to make sure there wasn't any waste. The module he would use was often four feet by eight feet, the size of a sheet of plywood. "I hate cutting plywood. I hate cutting any wood," he would say. "Why make a joist ten feet six inches? Dimensional lumber comes in two-foot increments. What are you going to do with that other foot and a half? Burn it? Put it in some landfill? Why the hell not use it? You paid for it. Nature's paid for it. Use it. It's good as free. Or make the goddamn joist ten feet instead of ten foot six. And, besides," he would say, "one of the most intelligent things the construction industry ever did was to make plywood and other sheet material four by eight. A double square. A perfect proportion to begin with. You can always go back to the square with that, four by four, two by two, one by one and never have a single scrap of wood left. They ought to make that a law. Teach it in every architecture school. If I ever see anyone in this office designing in anything less or more than two-foot increments, your future here is finished." His speeches were always so compelling and often repeated that I can recite most of them verbatim.

Robert wouldn't call himself a "green architect," but he was in principal. He believed in a lot of things that seem commonplace today. "Operating windows? Hell, the goddamn mechanical engineers did away with operating windows in the name of efficiency. They presume that the idiot occupants don't know that opening a window might screw up the balance in the HVAC system, so they seal the building tight as a drum. Hey, if I'm too hot, I just want to open a goddamn window and not wait for some mechanical device to tell me when it feels like making me comfortable." Robert would sometimes turn off the air-conditioning in the office if he was in a particularly petulant mood and run around opening all the windows, causing papers to blow off desks, and yelling for people to take their shirts off if they were too warm and besides put a paperweight on your papers; that was what paperweights were for. But there was no way of keeping the urban soot off our desks that would quickly accumulate when Robert would go into one of his frenzies. As soon as he would leave the office, Ms. Jones would close the windows and turn on the air.

"There are more than just people to think about in an office," she would say as she tried to sort out the papers blown from her desk onto the floor.

Robert would rant on in the office, sometimes raising his voice to a high pitch when he thought he was saying something important enough for everyone to hear, most often something everyone in Robert A. Michael's office had heard before, usually more than once.

When Andrew brought the suit against Robert, I knew that it was time for me to move on. It wasn't that I was legally implicated in anything. It was just that the atmosphere around the office was stifling. And there was no denying that I was intimately involved in the project and the fiasco, the disaster that could have been so much more disastrous. Thank God it wasn't. And as I said, Robert didn't blame or implicate me in any way. But all the same I thought as long as I was around, I would be a constant reminder to Robert and the office of this event, which they would rather forget. Ms. Jones tried to talk me out of leaving. They really needed someone with my dedication to being in the field, she said. But I knew that I had to return to school to develop some computer skills. Robert A. Michael and Associates was way behind in that area. Robert believed that he could solve that problem with one silver bullet. His name was Naut. I don't know his real name. He was just Naut, an animal kept in his gridded metal cage with his machines. He loved it. I knew I needed to know what he knew if I was ever going to be an architect in today's world.

As for Amy, she had their child during the design development stage of the project. I learned that she and Andrew jointly filed for divorce, putting their house on the market just a few years after the disastrous office party and deck incident.

MASOCHISM

The Architect's Alter Ego

Robert trusted me. When he was really depressed, I seemed to be the one he could most easily talk to. I wasn't an architect and was not a "professional" employee, though I knew as much about the operation of the office as anyone and could read Robert's mind when it came to business matters. As our relationship grew and time passed, he trusted me more and more implicitly with the office's operation, until one day when he was especially frustrated with the financial challenges facing the studio he said, "Ms. Jones, you run it. I just want to do the creative stuff." We didn't have any formal agreement. This wasn't a promotion. I admit that I was uncomfortable with the trust he was putting in me, especially as our financial picture got worse. To this day I don't understand his disappearance. Then again I had seen many of his bouts with depression.

I happened to be hired by Robert A. Michael and Associates, Architects during the same week that *Ms.* magazine began publication. Robert sarcastically called me Ms. Jones after he saw me carrying *Ms.* magazine into the office for my interview. He asked what it was. From that day on I was Ms. Jones. I usually went by the name K. T. Jones. Of course everyone would ask, "What's your full name?" I would have to tell them Katarina Thelissius Jankowitz; that is, if you went back to the name my parents gave me and the one that appears on my social security card and passport. My parents changed their last name to Jones and my first name to Katherine but didn't change my last name. K. T. was what they called me as a kid. I never knew whether it was for Katie, like in Katherine, or K. T. as short for Katherine Thelissius. My official name remains Katherine Thelissius Jankowitz. I spare the English-speaking world some pain by not using it.

My background is in art, with an MFA from Yale. Yeah, I know it sounds fancy—master of fine arts—but an MFA, even from Yale, isn't any more likely to make you an artist who can pay their own bills than a computer science degree from the local community college is likely to make you a computer geek zillionaire. Don't get me wrong. I had great teachers: the Albers, both of them; Cy Twombly as a TA. Our graduating class had a show in New York, and Rauschenberg and Warhol showed up along with their entourage, Rauschenberg because of his relationship with Twombly. And Warhol? I don't know, just because. Why did Warhol show up at anything other than to make the scene a scene?

Fortunately for me, I took up dancing as a second major. Another one of the underappreciated fine arts. Lucky me. But at least you might get a job as a dancer. Did you ever see an ad for "artist wanted"? No. But sometimes you'd see an ad for "dancer wanted." I saw one and answered it. I danced with Twyla Tharp when she was first getting started. I can't even remember if she paid me, but somehow we ate and slept out of the rain and had enough money to get back and forth between New York and her modest place upstate. She picked me out of the crowd, as they say. I think she liked me because I was big. I am a six-foot Polish big-boned broad with long arms, long legs, a skinny waist, and an ample chest and hips that disqualify many female dancers aspiring to dance in more traditional companies. Twyla's troupe of dancers looked different from each other. Not all the same uniformity required by so many companies. In that regard I fit right in. Twyla was terrific, and she tried to keep us employed year round, but dancing required a more masochistic lifestyle than I wanted to have.

If you didn't have a job in New York, then an option was to find someone with a job and sleep with them while you looked for a job. I found a guy to sleep with. He was a student of architecture attending the Columbia graduate program. He was a dedicated professional student. He had a bachelor's degree in philosophy and a master's and PhD in art history and couldn't find a job teaching. On the advice of his father, who still seemed to be supporting him, he entered Columbia's architecture program. He wasn't sure he liked it and didn't think his MArch promised any more job prospects than his PhD in art history. He worked part time for an artist. He drew plans for what she called her machines. Stella Dallas was the name she had given herself. She did these huge steel contraptions that were made at a local shipyard. My architect friend would take her doodles and turn them into drawings that he would then take to the shipyard, where he would supervise their fabrication at the docks. He seemed to like doing this more than going to school. We were, you might say, lovers, in that we shared the same two-room apartment and the same bed, though he was hardly ever in either. That was what caused the end of what might have been. He seemed to prefer not to sleep. I, on other hand, adored sleeping. He would come home to the apartment around 2:00 or 3:00 a.m. and want something to eat and to talk. My job was to feed and entertain him. I'd rather have entertained him in bed, but he always insisted that he was hungry. Scrambled eggs, bacon, and toast—I'm not sure he even realized I always served him the same thing. He made a point of getting home before it got light. He felt that as long as he got to sleep before it got light he would feel as though he had a full night's sleep. As a result, sometimes these breakfasts were rather rushed and he wouldn't want to make love because he had to get to sleep before it got light.

On the few occasions when he wasn't working, we would drift around the gallery scene. My friend had a knack for knowing where gallery openings were being held that had not been well announced. We were always welcome just to help fill up the space, and we added to the cool artistic ambiance in our hipster rags, he in black stovepipe jeans and me in a micro-mini skirt. I had put a red streak in my peroxide blonde hair, but I didn't really need that to be noticed. You get the picture, I think.

Truth is I never found a dancing job after my gig with Twyla. My, ummm, friend found an all-night eatery where he could get scrambled eggs, bacon, and toast and no longer needed my services in lieu of rent. I went home to Mom's to think this over and saw the ad in the paper while looking through the nonexistent "artist wanted" classifieds and instead found "architect's receptionist wanted."

Hey, close enough. I'd lived with and cooked breakfast for an architect. Surely that should qualify me for a position in an architect's office. It did. Robert was impressed that I had an MFA from Yale, which I guess to him signified that I had a certain level of intelligence and sophistication. He also seemed to vaguely recognize the name Twyla Tharp.

I recall Robert saying to me that I reminded him of the receptionist at SOM. First he had to explain SOM to me. A large corporate firm, he told me, not the size he aspired to, but its offices reflected a certain panache, the word he used. It began, he said, with the receptionist, tall, thin, and blonde in a white sheath dress sitting behind an all-white desk with a white phone and white roses in a white vase in an all-white room. I was to play the role of the tall, thin blonde. And so I did.

From this perch at the very front of the office, I had the privilege of observing all that went on. I didn't learn of Bentham's (I think that was his name) Panopticon, which really had nothing to do with the configuration of the office, until one of the new recruits pointed it out to me. The Panopticon allowed surveillance of whatever from a single position. I felt self-conscious about the power my physical position in the office ascribed to me as it gave me a view of the entire studio, except for Robert's office, which lodged he and his psyche.

I quickly learned that architecture is a culture not dissimilar to dance. Since I am not an artist except as defined by my degree and never got beyond the gallery culture of fine art, I can't compare art and architecture. But architecture, like dance, is masochistic. The work ethic is unbelievable. The two are about perfection. At least I can say that about the Robert A. Michael School of Architecture.

For instance, dance is both a solitary and a group endeavor. Dancers have their own thing to do as well as the obligation to be part of an ensemble. People play different roles. In that regard both architecture and dance are team sports. Of course everyone wants to be the star, and in both professions everyone is educated to believe they will be the star. But everyone can't be a star. The system can support just so many stars. Some of us forever play a supporting role. In Twyla's group we all felt like stars because we were all different and Twyla would choreograph different roles for us to play. They might be minor roles, but they were roles particularly suited to our talents. They were ours and ours alone. Robert's office was a lot like that. Robert seemed to have a knack for hiring people to play particular roles on his team.

When the boss is the choreographer and the principal dancer, director, and in charge of production, the star role goes to them every time. So it was never questioned that Robert A. Michael and Associates was headed by its principal Robert A. Michael just as Andy Warhol's Factory was headed by Andy Warhol, owner of the factory, its president, foreman, resident inventor/engineer, and creative director.

The star role was one of the things that led to Robert's problems. He couldn't give up the Robert A. Michael thing. In the years working for Robert I saw major changes in his financial situation, and while he was passing on some of the financial matters of the office to me he wasn't passing along financial control. Even there he wanted to be the star. When we talked about money, he would most frequently end our conversations by saying, "We don't have any problems that a little more work and a contract or two with reliable clients can't solve." End of subject.

Simply speaking, the outflow consistently exceeded the income. Why? Many reasons. For one, the cost of liability insurance kept creeping up. Some other small firms I've talked with are now just going cold turkey, figuring if they get sued big time, they will just go out of business. Everything is put in their spouse's name, which sometimes leads to a precarious relationship. Even though architects don't make much money, unfortunately for them they tend to marry others who don't make much money; for example, in no particular order, other architects, social workers, nurses, and even dancers. Lucky are the few who marry lawyers, bankers, or doctors or come from a wealthy clan. I offer this as an unverifiable anthropological study conducted by myself. Of course some might argue they know wealthy architects. They point out guys like I. M. Pei and Philip Johnson. They were born rich, though people think they became rich as architects. That's not true even though they probably made some money at their trade. Robert's not rich, though people think he is because he drives a Porsche. He used to own Porsches, but now he leases them as an office expense. He lives in a nice house, but that was built a long time ago before Abercrombie Heights' real estate prices went sky-high. He couldn't afford to build there now. His father, whose real estate firm sold half of Abercrombie Heights, helped him acquire the property, and his in-laws helped with the financing. The elder Mr. Michael made a ton of money in real estate that one might assume got passed on to Robert. But his father's three ex-wives, the ones after Robert's mother died, got to his estate first. They made sure of that.

Where was I? Oh, yes, the changes. Now we have FedEx charges never before imagined. Everyone wants things right away. And the equipment! Fax machines have morphed into high-speed computers, copiers, and printers that cost a bundle to maintain. We need health insurance and 401(k)s to help us keep our most valued employees, etc. We have these maintenance people in here all the time fixing stuff and the salesmen come right after them trying to sell us new stuff. The truth is that we are totally dependent upon this technology now. We have two of everything so if one breaks down we have another. It's the same as having two elevators or two exits from a building. Like NASA we operate with carefully considered backup systems. Robert is a fanatic when it comes to new stuff. That's why he insists that we lease rather than buy tech stuff so we can easily upgrade. Funny that a guy who wears the same Brooks Brothers clothes he wore in college and knows nothing about office technology wants this new stuff all the time, always looking for the next upgrade—just one of his many insecurities that is hurting our bottom line. What he needs is to upgrade his wardrobe. I've told him that.

I've talked with our accounting firm about controlling costs, and they say the trick is to pass more costs along to our clients. Pass along the FedEx expenses or if they want their drawings backed up electronically bill them for the disc, the printing time, the special staff time, and bill them for the extra billing. Learn from the lawyers, they say. Bill them for every minute you are on the phone with them.

Robert has a hard time with that. For one he doesn't value his time. "I know it," he says. "But how do I bill them for the idea I got in the shower this morning? It took me hours to draw that idea up, but the 'intuition' part just took a few seconds. It's taken me years to develop those intuitive skills. How do I bill for that? What is intuition anyway? It is just putting together the things you know, and it takes years of developing knowledge that contributes to good intuitive insights." Geez, he sounded like my art professors. "Nobody is born a genius." A favorite saying from both camps.

To make Robert know he wasn't the only one to feel this way, I told him about Bob Rauschenberg's idea of the artist taking a percentage of the increased value of a piece of art every time it is sold. As impossible as that might be, it was Rauschenberg's attempt to address the commodification of art that was occurring in the fine art world. Robert hadn't heard of that idea. He had $500,000 houses sell for a million and million dollar houses sell for two million years later. Robert is known as a signature architect. His name on a house increases its value. Not necessarily initially, but anyone who sells a Robert A. Michael house easily gets their architectural fees back and most likely a handsome profit to boot. But as one disgruntled client told me, every nickel of that so-called profit was deserved for the grief he and his wife had to put up with to get the fucking (his word) house built. He was a lawyer and had kept track of the hours they had spent arguing with Robert about what Robert considered "his" house. He and his wife built the house to save their marriage. It didn't. He said Robert should have paid for the divorce. I was sure he was going to sue Robert when his wife left him a month after they'd moved in. He was determined that she and Robert were having an affair. They weren't. I know. He sold the house a year later for half again as much as it cost him to build. "Some lucky son of a bitch is not going to have to go through the grief I had," he told me.

The business with the Darlings was the most difficult for Robert. It really tore him up. Just to keep this straight and so you're not embarrassed later, their name is pronounced Dahlings, not Darlings, as it is sometimes assumed. So darling, the Dahlings were real ball busters. To hear them tell it they are the most genteel people in town whose ancestry dates back to the day the Mayflower pulled up to a dock where the Chicago River meets Lake Michigan. And they may be right, except they are modern enough to hire ex-Nazis as their lawyers and the Mafia as their bookkeepers. The only time I've seen Robert cry was after a meeting with Mr. Dahling and his Nazi/Mafia henchmen. He came back to the office afterward. I was in the office catching up on some stuff after everyone else had left and in came Robert. He didn't even see me. He headed straight for the conference room that was the only closed room in the studio besides his office and opened the liquor cabinet hidden in the back of the console that no one but he and I knew about. I heard him sobbing as if he were having difficulty breathing. I popped my head in and said, "I'm here. How would it be if we went down the street and did some serious drinking?"

The office had a favorite bar down the street, Joe's Pub. Yeah, I know kind of generic sounding, and it was, filled with locals most of the time because the bartender knew when you needed a friend and when to leave well enough alone. And he knew your drinking habits, so every visit was like going home and having Dad mix your favorite something or other without having to ask. We are talking about a place that provided those basic creature comforts when you needed them most, a place where it took a few minutes for your eyes to adjust to the darkness.

Robert was pretty broken up. He and I had just had a meeting the day before over the books. I had insisted. Well, not really a meeting but one of the "sessions" where I'd say, "Robert we have to talk," and we would head into the conference room and close the door. Everyone in the office knew what we were going to talk about. It showed on our faces, the tension between us obvious, preceded by increased numbers of telephone calls easily discerned as being from bill collectors and intermittently frantic calls to clients. I knew this meeting with the Darlings was coming up, and I wanted Robert to know how desperate we were for him to get some money out of them. We'd put in all this work and hadn't received one single penny from them. "Robert . . ." I said. That's usually as far as I got in meetings like this. He didn't want to hear the details. "Just give me the bottom line," he would say. The answer at these sessions was almost always the same: "I don't have any more money, Robert, and tomorrow's payday and I can't squeeze any more out of the bank. The bottom line . . . is . . . we've reached the bottom."

Somehow, we would scrape through. A client would produce a check or Robert would call the bank and get our line of credit extended on the strength of a new contract. Robert liked to say, "Money happens." But money wasn't happening this month. The Darlings were the well we had to go to.

Robert just blurted it out: "KT . . ." In the bar he'd call me the more personal KT, reserving Ms. Jones for the office. "KT," now he said in a hushed tone, "there is no money coming from the Darlings. They made me take out our fee as a part of the action."

I didn't quite understand what he was saying. "What do you mean 'part of the action'?"

"I am a part owner in Darling Mews," he replied.

"Well, that's no big deal," I said. "We can take that to the bank for a loan."

"But I already have," he said, trying to keep his voice from breaking.

I felt double-crossed that he hadn't told me this before. As it turned out Robert had gone to the bank to get a loan on the strength of his contract with the Darlings. The bank saw this loan not as a business loan but as a personal loan because the deal was between the person Robert A. Michael and the Darlings. They based their loan on Robert's personal equity position in Darling Mews. "So, what's the big deal?" I said, trying to think of other angles. "You can just advance the studio a loan with that money and the office can pay you back . . . like you were the bank."

Robert stared blankly into the distance before turning his face toward mine. "I've already spent the money, KT. That is how I've paid for all those trips to New York."

Robert had lamented the trials of being an architect many times before as he and I sat at the bar at Joe's Pub, most often said within earshot of Joe, perhaps to explain Robert's miserly tips. Robert's monologue always began with a self-mocking matronly accent that would begin with something like "I would like to introduce you to my son the architect, who wasn't bright enough to become a doctor or lawyer like his brothers, but he was artistically gifted." At moments like this, Robert hated his dad for talking him into abandoning a career in art for one in architecture. Somehow Robert thought it would be nobler to be a starving artist than a starving architect. Said in the past tense, Robert would sound like a grieving mother at the deathbed or graveside of this beloved "other child." Robert was convincing at making this sound as if his mother were alive and he was the runt in a litter of successful professionals. Neither was true.

Robert's artistic abilities, his artistic goals, continuously haunted him and tended to set him against others of his profession. He found few other architects who shared his aesthetic commitment to the profession, a profession he still revered even though it couldn't pay his bills. "Why can't I forget all this aesthetic crap and just roll over and be the whore all my professional colleagues have become in order to survive? Architecture has been turned into a business. It's no longer an art form. Why do they even give out awards for how buildings look? Why bother? Show me a client who gives a flying fuck about what a building looks like and I'll show you a client who wants to be the architect."

Robert would rant on, and at this point I knew it was time to get him out of the bar and into a cab. His rap hadn't changed much since I first began working for him, but its meaning had shifted as he aged. As a successful young professional, he set himself apart from those less idealistic. As a seasoned professional, he would excuse himself for not having gotten a plum commission because of his ideals. And now, as a professional with what seemed to be the end of his career staring him in the face, he would lash out at Ayn Rand and Howard Roark, who had betrayed him.

One of the last times I saw Robert was after one of our sessions at Joe's that ended with my putting him in a taxi. I remember taking care of the tab and giving the taxi driver a healthy tip.

RECOGNITION

The Journalist

Robert by accident became my project. I was to become his publicist and marketing consultant as well as lover and inadvertently wife 2. I came to love Robert and supported his ambition to become a celebrity architect. But Robert had three strikes against him.

Strike One:

There was little doubt about the quality of Robert's product. His problem was that he was in the wrong market. Architecture from the Midwest simply had a hard time getting published. First of all there were fewer glamorous clients in the Midwest. To be published in *Architectural Digest* (later I learned referred to as *Architectural Disgust* by architects such as Robert), you not only had to have a big and photogenic domicile but you had to have an owner with a recognizable persona—star power. Besides a few people living along Chicago's Gold Coast or eastern shore or the hills of Colorado or the ranches of Texas and Montana, there was not much residential architecture of a high quality being created in the Midwest for celebrities the national media would recognize.

Strike Two:

The publishing industry resides largely on the East Coast. Writers, editors, and publishers would sometimes venture to the West Coast because it was exotic, the last cinematic version of the bourgeois lifestyle, and had a climate that celebrated indoor/outdoor living and top-down driving, and I would later appreciate flat roofs and slab on grade construction. But if you were an architect from the flyover part of the country and wanted to be published, you had to carefully plan your sojourn to New York, portfolio in hand, hoping that your appointments with the media crowd would not be broken and your trip would not be in vain, because you wouldn't be available to "come back tomorrow."

Strike Three:

It wasn't enough to do good work. Work you had done didn't count unless it had already received good reviews for one reason or another. It was the next project that got you the interview or the lunch date. No one wanted to talk to you about your last project. Journalists were always looking for the scoop. If you hadn't had lunch with Philip (Johnson) you were out of the loop. Even though Philip was originally from Cleveland that was soon forgotten even to him when he became a New York institution both in and out of architectural circles.

I met Robert while covering the PA design awards for Condé Nast. PA stood for *Progressive Architecture,* a professional journal famous for its annual awards program that recognized "the next great thing" in architectural design, research, and urban design. The awards were given at a "gala" lunch in a midtown hotel ballroom. There was little about the occasion that justified the term gala. A jury who reviewed submissions that were offered up anonymously identified the award winners. Attending the lunch were the winners, some of the jury members, clients, and friends, and sometimes a few of the who's who in the cloistered professional world of architecture.

The PA architecture awards were for work commissioned but not yet built. Each project supposedly had a client. Everyone suspected that some of the entries were more than a little fraudulent with make-believe clients, especially those entered from young as-yet-unrecognized firms.

Robert A. Michael did have a real client, and she was there with Robert. The project was a house and studio. The client was a painter. It was the kind of project that often received a PA award. It had a "poetic" program that left a large measure of aesthetic latitude to the architect. Awards, it seemed, generally went to houses both large and small, and also museums, churches, and sometimes a school or library. I learned residences were traditionally a subject where architects could try out new ideas. Many of the more innovative and might I say bizarre projects were prospective houses.

I was assigned to cover the affair even though I had never been to an architectural awards event before. My usual beat was museum and gallery openings. My task was to write an article that could be promoted among the publishers' "lifestyle" magazines in case something exciting happened. So be it.

The largest attraction for most architects who entered this awards program was the opportunity it provided to have their work published. In researching past awards issues of PA I found, however, that the jury's comments were not always flattering, a situation I found bizarre. But as I was also to learn more about the profession of architecture and architects' education, this self-imposed masochism seemed to explain itself.

So it was with Robert's "winning" entry for a live/work artist's space. The jury comments were almost all negative. For example, one juror commented, "I don't know what kind of work this artist produces, but it surely will not be helped if it is created in this studio." And another: "The architect totally misses the opportunity to have the live and work spaces integrated with each other." Robert seemed unfazed by the juror's comments, as were the other winners. They all seemed to bask in the glow of the attention they received in their few minutes of fame. As they were invited one by one to the stage with their client, a slide of their entry was projected on a screen behind them, and just as fast as they were welcomed on the stage they were ushered off with their paper citation inserted in a faux leather binder.

Robert's client was a thirty-something brunette with chiseled features and alabaster skin, wearing a deeply cut, cleavage-revealing, very business-like dark blue suit by Chanel. More the dress of a successful businesswoman than an artist, I thought. I was intrigued, thinking that this woman might be more than a starving artist and the trio—client, house, and architect—could make an interesting combination for a "style" piece. Robert's attire was nondescript, but that didn't matter. I became even more intrigued as the lights came down for the start of the presentations and the artist slipped her hand into his. *How cute*, I thought, even though Robert was at least a quarter century older than his client.

When the lights came up, I immediately headed for Robert's table. He and his client were engrossed in conversation. There seemed to be no one else at their table that they knew. I introduced myself. I don't remember much about the conversation other than giving Robert my card and asking him if I could call him to arrange an interview. He said sure but didn't even ask me who I was with and did not introduce his client, the artist, who someday might occupy this citation winning live/work artist's space that a juror said would not contribute to her artistic endeavors. Robert and his client seemed very anxious to get out of there. Robert now had his citation in one hand and his attractive client's hand in the other.

Robert wasn't anxiously awaiting my call. With the press of other assignments, it was nearly a month before I got to the PA project. I called Robert and reintroduced myself. He seemed only vaguely to remember meeting me and asked if I could call back later when he would have more time to talk. I called back later and found that he was out. I called again the next day. He apologized—it sounded genuine—and said that he had been called away from his studio unexpectedly. He had found my card. Yes, he did remember our conversation, and yes, he would be happy to talk with me. I really hated doing telephone interviews, which were always so impersonal, and I was going to be doing a layover in Chicago and wondered if I could meet him at O'Hare so I could interview him in person. It took some persuasion. I had to give him my whole bio, promise the article would be flattering, and go over in detail where it might be published. I told him there was no guarantee of its being published, but he was willing to take the time to talk with me.

We met in one of the bars at O'Hare Airport as previously arranged. The project that won a PA citation was already history, he informed me. His client was newly divorced, and the house/studio was to be her way of moving into the "art world thing," abandoning her career in banking. That partly explained the Chanel suite but hardly explained what she had been doing meanwhile. Robert told me that she met a fellow banker and was now newly married and had moved to San Francisco and had dropped the project. And, I thought to myself, she had dropped Robert as well. Robert didn't seem at all bothered by the fact that he'd lost the project and the artist and would-be lover, who was obviously a smooth operator to have accomplished this change in her life in a little more than a month.

I asked him how he felt about losing the project. He dismissed my question. "It happens all the time," he said. But once I engaged him in describing what he called the House/Studio Project I realized how important this project was to him. He gave me his client's name but said I couldn't use it in the article. I didn't tell him that my plan was to make the story about them and the house/studio, but of course that was no longer a possibility. That didn't stop him from describing the house/studio as a perfect client-architect relationship. Her needs were very vague, and she gave him a great deal of latitude to "express himself." The house didn't have a site. He'd made up the site for purposes of the submission to PA, but he assured me that this was a real project and that their intention was to look for a site once the design had been completed. That was contrary to everything Robert would tell me later about designing a house so it would fit a given site.

He produced a large black portfolio that contained the two pages from the PA publication that announced the winners of the PA design awards. Further back in the portfolio were a number of other drawings of the house/studio, many on tracing paper neatly mounted between plastic sheets. On the bottom right-hand corner of each were the letters RAM and a date. Then rather strangely, he began talking about how this house could make his client a great artist. If only she had stuck with him.

Eventually Robert informed me that he was separated from his wife and had been for years. The relationship with the artist had developed, as I suspected, into more than a professional relationship between architect and client. Robert told me that she had resented that he wanted to submit the house to PA for consideration in its awards program. "That's like putting your baby in a beauty contest," she had said. She had mixed feelings when he had won but agreed to go to New York with him to receive the award. They spent the rest of the day in their hotel room in a celebratory love fest. They parted the next morning, and that was the last he saw of her. He received a note in the mail on hotel letterhead from where they had celebrated receiving the award. It contained a check for the remainder due for his "services" along with a note that said, "Your ego is just too fucking big." Weeks later a friend in San Francisco sent him a wedding announcement from the *San Francisco Chronicle* declaring his client's marriage. Robert had seen this friend fairly recently and had told him about this client for the House/Studio Project and his infatuation with the artist client whose name the friend recognized in the oversized picture that accompanied the wedding announcement. There was no note sent to Robert by his friend, just the picture. A note was not needed.

I had never met a man who could so easily pour his soul out to someone he hardly knew, a stranger. Robert seemed not to have the filter that most people have that protects their true emotions from their expressed emotions. I wanted to change the subject. I didn't want to waste my time working on a story that had suddenly lost its substance. What could I salvage from this trip? Pretending I might still be interested in a story about his work, I fabricated the notion that I would have to see work of his that had actually been built before I could write a story, knowing there wouldn't be time before I had to catch my evening flight. We said good-bye, each saying; "We'll be in touch," in near unison.

I could explain to my publisher why my project had fallen apart and he would understand, so I put the thought of doing an article on Robert's architecture out of my head. That wasn't the kind of journalism I did. But to my surprise I received a call from Robert shortly after my return to New York asking when I could visit so he could show me his work. I was embarrassed that Robert took my suggestion of seeing some of his work literally when it was only meant as a kind gesture. I felt sorry for the guy but with a sense of obligation since he had assumed my request was genuine. The opportunity to be published was dangling in front of him.

I arrived at O'Hare on a Monday morning. I was surprised when he said he would pick me up, presuming that some underling would do so and perhaps even show me some of the houses before I met Robert. But there was Robert to greet me. To lower Robert's expectations for this visit, I once again told him that architecture wasn't my beat—lifestyle was—and he would have to explain the architectural merits of what he showed me. He said he understood.

We headed for Abercrombie Heights, a misnomer if there ever was one, but despite its less-than-heroic heights the area did offer surprising views over Lake Michigan and the city. We looked at four houses varying in age from thirty to two years old. The two-year-old house had been a teardown. An older house, if forty years is older for a house, was bought by the owner for close to a million dollars to make way for a new house by Robert. Robert had known the architect of the original house. Even though he was proud of what he had done or he wouldn't be showing me this house, he was embarrassed that he had been party to having a colleague's house demolished. His remorse seemed genuine. It all began, he said, when he had made a disparaging remark about having to add on to the original house. The client tore it down without telling him because they wanted him to have greater freedom in creating his own design. He said he hadn't meant his comments the way they had been taken and never anticipated they would tear down the original that fit the site so well. "Thank goodness," Robert said, "the poor goddamn son of a bitch who had designed the teardown was dead and will never know." But he got a note from the architect's widow when she found out, and she was on several museum boards that could make matters difficult if she wanted to make Robert's involvement in desecrating her husband's landmark work a cause célebre.

Robert's houses all had his signature. They floated, they were transparent, they "celebrated the horizon," as he put it, and they were without what he called ornament but were beautifully detailed "in a minimalist way." As he pointed out, "It's all about how you turn the corner." I wasn't sure what that meant. But the thing that struck me most as we walked about was that his only commentary about the houses was negative, the backstory, as it were. "We should have put the fireplace against that wall rather than over there . . . The kitchen was supposed to be open, but she didn't want anyone to see her cooking . . . The bathroom was so goddamn huge it took up half the budget for the house, what a waste . . . They really didn't need three garages, and it ruined the proportions." What did I know? They all looked wonderful to me, but here was Robert systematically running each one of them down.

The tour was compact, but even so it was 1:00 p.m. by the time we got to his office. He introduced me to Ms. Jones and asked if I could wait for lunch while he made some phone calls. Ms. Jones felt obliged to entertain me and started by showing me all the awards Robert A. Michael and Associates had won. The PA citation was already prominently displayed matted within a black frame like all the other awards. She took me into the studio and walked me around, pointing out this project and that, not introducing me to anyone as everyone who was there seemed totally engaged in what they were doing, except for a guy who had one hand wrapped around a sandwich and the other on a mouse. Ms. Jones explained that he was the cybernaut testing some new software for the office.

We returned to the reception area, and Ms. Jones invited me to sit down whereupon she told me her life story. She calculated the time she had allotted for this quite accurately, for she was just finishing how she had been employed by Robert by luckily being in the right place at the right time when Robert emerged from his office. She had even shared the source of her title, Ms. Jones.

Robert's office and the conference room were the only spaces with doors. He asked me to come into his office and shut the door. "How much time do you have?" he asked. I replied that I had planned to spend the day and would be leaving on an early flight out of O'Hare tomorrow. "Good, we can have dinner together" was his response. This sounded more like a command than an invitation. I demurred and said that I should begin writing but with a hesitancy that said, "Ask me again." He did. The hotel was just a few blocks away. He allowed that I could begin writing and then we could have a nice dinner together and talk some more. But by now I was hungry, as it was nearly two, three New York time. Just then Ms. Jones opened the door holding a tray of sandwiches and a couple of sodas. This didn't fit my salad-for-lunch diet, but I took one of the sandwiches while Robert gave me the history of the firm. And, he told me about his father, his son and daughter, the death of another son, and his wife, who had left to spend some time in Santa Fe with friends while they got their heads together. He didn't think they would. He would be by the hotel to get me at 8:00 p.m.

Robert arrived about 8:15 and phoned from the lobby saying that he would wait for me in the bar. I was ready, but by the time I arrived at the bar, Robert had already ordered a martini. He asked what I wanted. If he was going to start by drinking martinis, I was not going to be shy. I asked for a shot of Stoli with a twist and a glass of water.

Robert was handsome, though he seemed to want to conceal his good looks in the awful clothes he wore. Everything he had on seemed at least a decade too old. Could you even buy clothes like this any longer—a tweed jacket, an oxford button-down shirt with a rep tie, khaki slacks, and plain-toed cordovan shoes? We sat at the corner of the bar, nursing our drinks. Robert said he hadn't been able to get a reservation until 9:30 and immediately swallowed the rest of his martini and asked if I would like another. Our conversation was small talk. Robert finally got around to asking me about me. What did I do? How long had I done it? Where was I born? Where had I gone to school? Was I married? Did I have children? The answers to these predictable questions came from me in short bursts. I was a writer. For twenty years. I was born in Cleveland Heights, Ohio (another heights, I thought; how strange), and went to Smith. I had been married (holding up my naked ring finger to emphasize the past tense—why did I do that?). I had a son who was twenty and wouldn't speak to me. If Robert did his math, he would calculate that I was someone in their mid—to late forties, and he would be right.

Shortly before 9:30, we went out the front door of the hotel where his Porsche was sitting with its top down under the watchful eye of the doorman. The doorman seemed relieved that Robert had arrived to retrieve the car and obviously pleased with the tip Robert had given him. As we drove away, Robert said, "In certain places there is nothing that a Porsche and a sizable tip can't get you." I was reminded of a famous male Hollywood star who had recently been arrested for public indecency on the Sunset Strip for soliciting a prostitute who gave him a blow job in public before he could pull away from the curb. He was driving a Porsche. I suppressed my urge to tell this story.

We headed north and just before reaching a sign that said Abercrombie Heights pulled under the porte cochere of a French bistro with valet parking. The young man who approached the car immediately said, "Hello, Mr. Michael," and then turned to me and said, "Hello, Miss," obviously recognizing that I was not Robert's wife. I wondered how many "Hello, Misses" Robert had brought to this place. The valet hopped into the car, the motor still running with a purr, and moved it ahead into a spot marked "no parking" in front of the restaurant, a space obviously used as the restaurant's billboard and reserved for Porsches or better, but what could be better than that silver bullet that seemed able to fly.

Robert knew the maître d', who welcomed Robert with a vigorous handshake. "Hello, Mr. Michael, let me show you to your table." The emphasis was on "your" with the sense of ownership one has when saying your house, your daughter, your fortune, and your wife, though none of that was said. I was getting the feeling that Robert was quite well off even if his office appeared a little frayed at the edges. The dinner was delicious, though I only vaguely recall what we had. Extraordinary wines, a white with the mussels and a red with the duck—I think. Before we were finished with the duck, Robert said, "I've saved the best for last. I want you to see my house. It's best at night and has a fantastic view of the city. Would you join me for an after-dinner drink there?" This explained why we were eating near Abercrombie Heights rather than downtown or near my hotel or the airport. Why hadn't Robert shown me his house during the day and saved it for this evening? The narrative Robert was creating seemed quite obvious now.

We didn't tarry after dinner. The drive itself was quite beautiful, and even though it had become cooler, Robert kept the top down so we could enjoy the clear sky and the air, which seemed to get cleaner as we drove through Abercrombie Heights, or was it Mont Abercrombie? The pretension seemed to wear off as I realized how spectacular the view of the city was from there with its light show of hyperkinetic white, red, and green dots all moving in sequence on one side and a vast hole of blackness on the other side, the endless expanse of Lake Michigan disappearing on the horizon.

Robert abruptly pulled into a drive whose massive iron gates opened as if at his command. The gates closed behind us as I thought, *Robert now has his prey.* We climbed a bit more, and at the crest of the hill lying before us was a floating transparency of a house shimmering on the horizon, a house so dematerialized that the sophistication of the other houses I had seen that day were totally overshadowed here. There were just two shimmering planes that allowed the nearly invisible horizon to separate them, the one at the bottom black, the one above white. The stars that studded the heavens formed a blanket that covered and united the entire scene. This was magic.

I was floating. Robert brought me a Stoli like I had ordered at the hotel bar so long ago. He poured a brandy for himself and motioned me outside and down a flight of stairs to sit by a pool that was defined only by the reflection of starlight suspended in a black matrix of water.

I was truly blown away. Robert smiled, seeing my astonishment. I wanted just to soak it all in but felt the need to say something as my mind raced ahead trying to understand the feeling that had overcome me. "Robert," I said, "I want to be your publicist. Your work has to be known. It is awesome. I know those are corny words. I can do better. Let me write about you. Let me write about your work."

Robert said, "What a splendid offer. I accept. Shall we adjourn to the bedroom and consummate the deal?" No answer was necessary—no handshake. What better way to see the rest of the house?

CONNECTIONS

The Publicist

Robert was now my project. According to Robert, a partner at Skidmore, Owings & Merrill, his former employer from long ago, during the few months he worked there, told him there were just three opportunities for one to have an architectural practice. The first was to be born rich. The second was to marry rich. The third was to become a partner in a corporate firm like SOM. Robert didn't believe that scenario. There was a fourth way, he believed. He had created an office that had survived two recessions. It could survive a third. He thought he just needed to get his work publicized.

I'm not sure whether this is the same scenario that brought the Finish/American architect Eero Saarinen together with his second wife, Aline Bernstein, who was a New York journalist and author doing freelance work and employed as an editor at the *New York Times*. Saarinen, like Robert, dwelt in the flyover backwaters of the Midwest, Detroit in this case. Actually his office was in the Detroit suburb of Bloomfield Hills. Aline was assigned to write an article for the *New York Times Magazine* on the innovative GM Tech Center also located in a Detroit suburb, which was designed by the Saarinen office. Are you beginning to see some similarities here? They were later married. The friend that told me this real tale of infatuation and love described it as a Cinderella story.

Sometimes when you look back to particular events or circumstances that have deeply affected your life, it is easy to confuse the event you planned with the event that occurred and the event you recall. So it was with my becoming involved with Robert. I am not the kind of woman to become infatuated or to use that old cliché "fall in love." I believe I have a healthy cynicism concerning the male ego. But my relationship with Robert seemed preordained after our first meeting at the PA awards luncheon. I am also not impulsive, and I am not, I don't think, calculating. Looking back on our first dinner date and the proposal I made to become his publicist, which led to a tacit agreement and a night of lovemaking as a way of confirming our agreement, it seemed like an event I had planned, which happened and which I seem to recall in vivid detail. But it was Robert who invited me to his fabulous house for after-dinner drinks. He was an equal partner in this unspoken conspiracy. The opening scene of our relationship is the same from multiple perspectives.

I would be shortchanging myself to imagine that Robert was only attracted to me because I had access to the East Coast publishing world. I am, after all, an attractive willowy brunette who although in my mid-forties can still turn a head. New York, despite the pressure it delivers to anyone who works or lives there, is a good place to stay young, a place where you have to stay young.

I did complete the article on the PA award winners. I confined myself to just PA's residential project winners, three of them, and interviewed each. Robert had the balls to ask if I had laid each of my interviewees. I didn't dignify his question with a reply. I did remind him that one of the others was a woman and that wasn't my game and asked who he thought had laid whom that night in his transparent and levitated house that celebrated the horizon.

I wrote versions of the article that featured each of the PA entries separately. None of the professional journals wanted the articles, of course. The PA awards were already tied to a promotion by one magazine. Why would competing journals want to promote this venture? PA had already milked the newsworthiness of the awards, and nothing more would get published about these projects unless another award was won. Robert seemed not to understand.

But friends at *Elle* thought Robert's own house, which I had pictures of, might make a good location for a fashion shoot. Robert was furious with me. "Goddamn," he said. "*Elle*? What screwed-up vain little bitch reading *Elle* is going to ever hire me as an architect? If you were going to solicit the vanity press, then why not go to *Vanity Fair*? At least adults read that magazine."

I was furious right back. "Look, Mr. Self-righteous. If you are published, just hope the writer spells your name right. If you want better PR, go get yourself mugged. That might make the front page of the *Post*. The more beat-up, the better. They might even note that you're an architect from out of town. Anything to feed people's paranoia about the city that will grab their readers' attention. Why bother with this professional magazine shit? Do you think anyone who reads an architectural journal is going to hire you? No. Their readers are just a bunch of white male architects with penis envy measuring each other's column inches. Hey, maybe one of the screwed-up vain little bitches who read *Elle* will want to introduce you to her mother when she's finished reading the article." This put an end to our first serious conversation about my role in Robert's professional life.

We began to see each other regularly. He would make excuses to come to New York, and we spent long weekends together. He told his office he was courting a client. It was between his second and third martini on one of those weekend nights that he informed me that his wife had asked for a divorce. He seemed irritated when he told me. I suspect by telling me he wondered what that might do to our uncomplicated sex-driven relationship. Would our relationship now have to become more serious since he was unburdened of his marital status? I thought that would have to be his choice.

This looked to be just another torrid weekend in New York. But Saturday afternoon we decided to go see a show at the Museum of Modern Art. It was the deconstruction show. "You know," he said to me, "I don't know what makes these guys so interesting. So they've discovered non-Euclidean geometry and called it a commentary on today's chaotic society. They got the Frenchman Derida to bless them, or did he invent them? I'm not sure who invented whom. Then Johnson joined in to promote this new architectural phenomenon. Johnson wrote the book on the International Style and killed modernism. Was he just looking for something new to blow up?"

Robert hated postmodernism, a so-called movement that he thought was simply eye candy applied to a lot of modernist tenets. But Robert thought the decon crowd was truly subversive. Jack Derrida, Jameson, Benjamin—what did these people have to do with architecture? Zaha Hadid had won the Peaks competition handpicked by Johnson, he thought, and the world seemed to come apart after that. The students he had met recently couldn't even draw a right angle. "This sucks."

Robert wasn't very talkative normally. He had a hard time putting words together at times, especially when he got emotional. I thought perhaps he had dyslexia. This showed up in the notes he wrote me as well where letters in his words would be interchanged. To calm him down I decided to invite him back to my place, three rooms and a kitchen on the West Side, close to Central Park. I'd lived there for ten years since my divorce, all of those years with my son Conrad, whom I eventually learned despised me. When he left for Brown, he said he never wanted to see or talk to me again. I didn't know what to make of it. I thought the move was up to him. I only hear from him a few times a year, and sometimes he drops in like he never left. I think to see if he still has a room in New York. His father has told me he dropped out of Brown after his first year and headed for India. He gets postcards from various places in Southeast Asia. Supposedly Conrad works as a merchant seaman, but his father isn't certain.

Conrad's room is still his room, largely untouched. I thought he should feel welcome when he comes back. I got rid of his bunk bed, which was constructed as a bed on the top and a worktable below, and bought a hideaway to replace it. His photographs were still on the wall. An odd assortment of subjects, mostly black-and-white pictures he had taken himself and some that he had purchased. His favorite subject was the neighborhood. Anything busted up grabbed his attention: battered cars, graffiti, broken fences, dead animals, waste that collected in doorways, old tattered signs, architectural details. Our neighborhood was not a bad neighborhood, but if you judged it from Conrad's photos, you would think otherwise. I hadn't thought of his pictures as being particularly morbid until after he left and I became his curator, as it were, and could see them as a complete body of work. I couldn't throw them away or even take them off the wall where Conrad had arranged them. This was Conrad's gallery. Metal boxes stored his carefully labeled prints and negatives. He asked to build a darkroom in a little pantry off the kitchen. I said no, an emphatic no that further drove a wedge between us. He used a neighbor's darkroom to do his developing and printing. A nice old guy who had lived in our building forever under rent control showed Conrad how to use his equipment and taught him tricks of the trade. As a teenager, when Conrad most needed a male mentor, this guy who was at least in his sixties took over where his father left off. I never knew his name and hadn't met him until after Conrad left for Brown. One day he introduced himself to me in the lobby, saying, "Hi, I am Isaac, Conrad's photography friend. How's he doing?"

Embarrassed, I said, "Just fine," and then talked about the weather or some dumb thing just to change the subject. It was nearly a year later before I confessed to Isaac, whom I now seemed to run into regularly, that I hadn't heard from my son and only knew he was doing okay because his father kept me informed.

I think that when Robert walked into my place, he could sense the presence of a man. It didn't have the telltale signs of being occupied by a woman, the knitted throw draped over the back of the couch that was occupied by dozens of pillows, curtains in the window, etc. Most of my furniture wouldn't look bad in one of Robert's houses. My living room was mostly decorated, if that's the proper word, with some of Conrad's pictures along with photographs by Richard Avedon and Aaron Siskind, which were hung in places of honor—by themselves. On the side table next to the couch, I kept a picture of my ex and Conrad taken when Conrad was about eight, the year Max and I parted company. I hardly looked at the picture any longer, but it had become a fixture that I couldn't imagine moving. Like most women, my life was perceived to only have begun once I got married. When I told people that Max was in "theater," nothing more had to be said about the divorce. Marrying someone in the "theater" was risky business and attempted only by the foolhardy. I had never told anyone that Max had left me for a man. No one could pull that out of me.

Robert saw the picture on the table and said, "What a handsome family; when was that taken?" It was one of those throwaway questions that tried to disguise Robert's discomfort in this alien environment. He turned his attention to the pictures on the wall. "Who took these pictures? Your husband?"

I began to respond, "This one is by Richard Avedon and—"

"Yes, I know, and that one is by Aaron Siskind, but who took the others?"

"They were taken by my son."

"An exceptional talent," Robert responded, with genuine enthusiasm in his voice.

I didn't feel like talking about my son, or my husband, or my life, and so I tried to move the subject away from Conrad's photos. "Everybody knows Richard Avedon, but how do you know Aaron Siskind?" I asked.

"How do you know Aaron Siskind is a better question?" he said.

"My son saw this picture in a gallery in SoHo and could speak of nothing else. I splurged and bought it for his sixteenth birthday. I thought he would want to take it with him to school. But no. He said, 'You bought it. It's yours. It will increase in value.' I am planning to travel light." *Shit,* I thought to myself. *Here I am trying to change the subject and I start talking about my son again.*

"Has he ever taken architectural photographs?" Robert asked.

"Not while he lived with me," I said. "But you've avoided my question. How do you know Aaron Siskind?"

"He was part of the Chicago . . . the New Bauhaus. He saw the world through fresh eyes with all its warts and scars." Robert's voice trailed off as though he was remembering something important. "If only I had been older and able to study with Moholy-Nagy and Mies and Chermayeff when Siskind was teaching in Chicago. Sometimes I fantasize about how my career would have been different if . . ." and Robert slipped back into his wistful thoughts.

ARCHITECTURE, PORNOGRAPHY, FASHION

The Photographer

Mother introduced me to Robert on a visit I made to her apartment to pick up my camera equipment shortly after I returned to New York. I hadn't lived at Mother's since I entered college. She had told me that Robert was an architect. They were friends. After our introduction and small talk, she interjected that he might need a photographer to document some of his projects. He looked a little surprised. I thought this might be a way of restarting my nascent career as a photographer. Robert and I left Medea's (mother hated being called Mother or Mom; I think she hated being a mother) to go to a bar down the street, my first visit since returning to New York to this familiar neighborhood establishment that had tolerated my underage drinking.

I had spent some time at the New York Public Library when Medea suggested that she might have a job for me as an architectural photographer, but she hadn't mentioned Robert. A photographer whose work I discovered at the library was Judith Turner. To me her pictures of architecture were pornographic snapshots, abstractions, depending upon your frame of mind. Just as Edward Weston looked at the female body through his lens as studies in abstract form, so too Turner was able to look at architectural form as both voyeur and artist. I didn't tell Robert that I had done some work in pornography in college, behind a camera, not in front of it. It was just a way to make a buck. But I got so I became interested in the abstraction of lovemaking, how a detail could be made erotic. Two bodies fucking—big deal. But a hand on flesh, a knee, an elbow, a breast, or buttocks could be photographed to take on an erotic vibe. A rocking motion of a body fragment exaggerated because of the closeness of the lens to the subject could become an erotic detail that left to the imagination the rest of the narrative. The texture of skin, hair, sweat—these were the things that told one more about the act, made up more of a story than a dead-on wide-angle view of the couple on the bed in a motel room. My stuff got some quizzical looks. But it found an outlet. I told Robert about my interest in detail, which he said he had already gathered from looking at the photographs that hung on Medea's walls. "The idea for a building sometimes begins with a detail," Robert said. We were immediately on the same page, and we hadn't yet gotten to our second drink.

Architecture doesn't move, but the things around it do, and I decided that a lot of good architectural photography is about being in the right place at the right time or creating the right place. Photographer

Julius Schulman performed magic with the people he included in his most celebrated architectural photographs. He made people a part of the architecture, a significant detail that said so much about his real subject the space they occupied. The Case Study House No. 22 in Los Angeles, suspended on a Hollywood hill with the city like a canvas below, and inside the house, two women, one sitting on a couch supporting her head with her arm on its back and the other, a teenager, perhaps a daughter or young friend, holding her hands in her lap, the two having a conversation as they appeared suspended over LA with their backs to this amazing cinematic view. One had the sense, the composition so perfect, that if either of them moved the house might tumble into the valley below. Likewise his picture of a Neutra house in Palm Springs, California, created its own narrative. All that was shown was a corner of the house by the outdoor pool with light coming out of the house, and there on the left next to the pool was a reclining figure doing a perfect imitation of a Henry Moore sculpture. Schulman was a storyteller. Photographs make us believe we are looking at reality, but we are most often tricked by the photographer. Schulman used infrared film to enhance his photographs. He could manipulate the character of a photo, not the composition, unless he decided to crop a photo, but the character of a photo, in his darkroom. He said himself that his job was "not to glamorize but to glorify . . . making the building look better than it really is." Like architects, better photographers like to create illusions.

I believe that architecture, pornography, and fashion photography are all related. Take pornography. If you met the actors on the street in normal attire you would be unlikely to identify them as porn stars. Similarly, some buildings you might pass by and never take notice of unless some photographer had used them as a subject. Take Bill Hedrich's iconic photo of Frank Lloyd Wright's house in a faraway place in Pennsylvania, Falling Water, for example. In Hedrich's photo the falls over which the house is built were photographed with a slow shutter speed and recorded as a gossamer veil falling like a skirt below the extended bosom of the house itself. Hedrich's photo of Falling Water is one of the most famous architectural shots of all time taken from a vantage point few people will see unless they have a vivid memory of Hedrich's photo and get off the well-beaten tourist path. I would say this photograph was so perfectly framed by the lens of a camera that the house itself can never live up to the expectations this photograph creates. The iconic shot. Just as the photo of Marilyn Monroe with her skirt flying up to expose her legs up to her crotch as she stood over a New York subway grate made her the blonde bombshell. Photographs made Wright the iconic architect and Marilyn the iconic American female. Both photos captured through the lens of a camera, images that were revealed by a photographer's artistic vision.

Robert and I continue to have a long discussion about photography and architecture. I insisted that photography was not about reality but about illusion. He denied that illusion was part of his work, but from what Medea told me about his house he was either being dishonest or was naive about his own work or for some reason was in denial about what mother thought was the most important aspect of his designs. I asked him why people chose to have architects design residences for themselves if it wasn't to create a grand illusion, their own illusion, about who they were. We went on like this. Then suddenly Robert agreed with me. He confessed that he felt that the reason most people did not want to deal with architects is that it forced them to imagine and then confront who they were.

I recall that he used an interesting analogy. "Why don't people order custom-made clothes anymore?" he asked. "Because they have to decide who they are first. For instance," he exclaimed, "something as simple as a tailor-made suit requires you to pick out a fabric, the cut, shape of the lapel, cuffs or not, how much break in the pants, how many pleats or none, number and location of pockets inside and out, a vest, all monumental decisions put forth by the tailor and a nightmare for the identity challenged. But if you go to the rack, you can immediately put on a garment, walk around, look in the mirror, and in a short time decide 'that's me' without ever having to make the time-demanding and highly charged decisions about what constitutes the suit you are about to commission, not sure that all those decisions actually come together so you can say 'that's me.' Custom designing for most people is a scary challenge unless they have a high degree of self-confidence, which immediately puts them at odds with the tailor or the architect who feel they are empowered to act in their client's best interest—creating the proper illusion."

Robert carried on. In a short time I realized that Robert was feeling conflicted about designing for a mass market—the great unwashed. On our third drink he began talking about Darling Mews, at once prideful he had been asked to design such a large project and yet disdainful of its objectives. He didn't want to be the Martha Stewart of architecture, he lamented. Mitch Darling, the developer of Darling Mews, was creating this internal conflict for Robert, his architect. Robert wanted to create a design that would allow people to make choices. But, he said, Mitch Darling had other ideas. He had told Robert that people would not be moving into Darling Mews because they wanted to make choices. They wanted the developers of Darling Mews to tell them what was right, what was appropriate, what other people wanted, and what would assure them of a fair return on their investment. Mitch had suggested to Robert that they should go into the business of designing sheets and pillowcases, "Do the whole thing." Robert went on, mimicking Mitch Darling. "We could have our own big-box store on the edge of Darling Mews where everyone would have to buy their housewares and hardware and software and not have to make anything except petty decisions about their lifestyle. Eliminate the constant fear of being incorrect. That was the job of Darling Mews, to eliminate the fear that its inhabitants might be incorrect or, even worse, live next to someone who might be incorrect." No mention of the Stepford wives, but I could tell that Robert was torn by this image of superficial correctness. He went on in his own words as he struggled with both the high—and low-mindedness of this proposition of working for the Darlings. In a defensive tone I recall him saying, "After all, the Bauhaus believed in total design. The architect should design everything. And wasn't it Mies who got in trouble with Dr. Farnsworth because he wanted to select her furniture and even tell her where it had to be placed in his masterpiece?" But Darling Mews was something else. It was becoming manufactured taste. Martha Stewart, Ralph Lauren, Laura Ashley (what ever happened to her?). Not taste born of a movement or born of a philosophy or born of a passion. Architecture commoditized. No, it was just made up taste, the way new cereals are created by changing the formula with salt and sugar and added color.

But it wasn't Darling Mews Robert wanted me to photograph. It might not even be built, he said with no signs of remorse. It was his house. Robert's house! The sum total of his life, as it were, he told me, even though it was the first house he designed after the spec houses he had done for his father. As I learned at Brown, for so many artists and architects of genius, their first work is the most brilliant and they spend the rest of their life trying to capture that moment of greatness. Every idea, every move, every nuance of architectural art had been tested on his spec houses, houses that began in his father's imagination for imaginary clients that gave Robert the latitude to test his ideas without encumbrances. Robert was the architect, client, and owner for Robert's house. The house remained as he had envisioned it. Robert's first wife understood that she and the children would play no role in the design of this house even though they may occupy it if they behaved properly. Robert's first wife was no Stepford wife; then again she could have become one if she had remained married to Robert.

Robert and I agreed that we would begin my photography project starting with a photo essay of Robert's house. That way I would become familiar with what he described as his architectural vocabulary helping to inform me as to how to photograph his other work. He seemed most interested in recording his house for posterity in a way that best reflected his vision. I was happy to help him achieve that goal.

Robert was going to spend a week in New York, and that would be an ideal time for me to live in the house with my Hasselblad and Nikon, lights, light meter, and lots of film. I wasn't to move the furniture; he would have it properly arranged before he left. I hoped for sun and rain and fog and clear starry nights and the possibility of skinny-dipping in the pool that Medea told me she loved so much.

RITUAL HAZING'S

The Student

I first met Robert when he was a critic on our final semester project. Architectural "juries" in college are ritual hazing's. Besides the faculty, professionals are invited to participate, usually friends of the faculty and sometimes faculty from other schools. At the conclusion of an assigned project, students "pin up," their work to be evaluated in these critiques or crits or juries sometimes called reviews.

Robert A. Michael seemed dumbfounded to see a black girl pin up in front of him. He looked at me like I was some kind of help. He seemed embarrassed. For himself or for me? I didn't know. Not once did he address me. He asked questions as though they were being asked to the wall, or the other critics. He pointed at my drawings and asked a question and then waited . . . as though he was half expecting that the drawings would speak . . . they would talk and he wouldn't have to talk with me.

Yeah, I think he was uncomfortable. Real uncomfortable. I think he would be uncomfortable in front of any woman, but a black woman wanting to be an architect. Wow! That was out of his field of vision. Way outside.

To avoid being trapped like a deer in the high beam of the jury, who often acted as though they were in a grudge fight with each other, students took the initiative by playing the role of provocateur, though few had the courage or would take the risk. An article in the *Harvard Design Magazine* edited by two GSD graduates credited their classmates with contributing 109 "strategies" for surviving a jury. Those 109 strategies obviously came from the minds of men intended to distract the reviewers. My strategies, unpublished, were decidedly feminine.

I wasn't a ravishing beauty, but then again you wouldn't be surprised to see my picture in *Ebony* magazine. I knew how to use my good looks. I had several "strategies" to distract the jurors and to keep them from attacking my project or me. Most students felt that attacking a project was the same as attacking its author, leaving the student totally humiliated. One of my strategies was to make a point regarding my design by leaning over the model I had constructed to illustrate my project. I made sure the model was on the table in front of me, between me and jury members. What one wore to the jury was critical, a design problem in its own right. For some women, the risk takers, it was cool to wear something that was going to show some cleavage. My breasts are small, but they are breasts. I didn't wear a bra, and my favorite white scoop-necked blouse contrasted nicely with my chocolate-colored skin and showed cleavage. I put on some body lotion so I had a nice sheen, and my skin was clear. My classmates called me the Nubian Queen. Why not? I might have been.

When I presented, like everyone else I got excited. It was kind of a sexual thing, being up in front of everybody. Kinda on display. Sometimes it made me imagine what it might have been like to be a slave at auction. But I wasn't for sale, and this white guy who was supposed to be talking about my project couldn't even talk with *me* about it. Was he afraid to look? The excitement causes my nipples to get erect. It used to embarrass the hell out of me. But now I know what an effective tool the erect nipple can be. I wore the rayon top with a scoop neck, not too deep and not too high, so my tits showed only when I wanted them to. I'd reach across my drawings pinned to the wall to point out something on the opposite side, and with my blouse tucked into my skirt the blouse with tight sleeves would go taut across my body like a tensile skin structure. Out popped the nipples. I didn't have to look. I could feel those eyes. They never looked at the drawing. They weren't supposed to.

So between stretching to point out details in the drawings and bending over to point out things in the model, I gave the jury a pretty good show. Often this led to blank expressions and a clumsy silence, and when I finished, I would have to say, "Do you have any questions? I can go on."

After reading the *Harvard Design Magazine* piece I realized that female students have a decided advantage in distracting juries from their work when the jury is most often male, I would say 90 percent of the time—male. Bear with me as I reveal another trick. That is the leg trick. This needs a chair, and I didn't have one at this review. But if there is a chair around, you can claim exhaustion, because everyone knows you've been up all night, or for two or three nights, and you are about to collapse. Victorian women had this trick down pat, and they would feign fainting. So you grab a chair. You place the chair in front of you. Then you sit on the edge of the chair and cross your legs, making a big swinging motion with your outstretched leg to get the jury's attention. Then you move forward in the chair, which causes your skirt to ride up your thigh. Then you say, "Do you have any questions? I can go on." Legs can get them just like erect nipples. It helps to have legs like Tina Turner or Sharon Stone's. For a tutorial just watch their movies.

So there I was, the Black Bitch Nubian Queen Architecture Wannabe, explaining her stuff to this white guy who couldn't look her in the eyes. The comments were short and were mostly from the faculty who knew me, loved me, and weren't the least intimidated by *me.*

I like to think that Robert must have gone home and thought about me a long time after that jury. He called me the next day. I don't know how he got my number—from one of the faculty he knew, I guess. He needed someone to work for him. They had just gotten a new contract for a church job, and he wondered, since this last project at school was just finished, if I could come in for a few hours a week and do some drawings for them and maybe help make a model. Robert A. Michael was a decent architect; otherwise he wouldn't have been invited to the crit. He was someone the faculty respected. He had a reputation for having a big ego . . . what architect doesn't? He works hard . . . what architect doesn't? But how was he going to work with this Black Bitch Nubian Queen who wanted to be an architect? And why me, this woman he could hardly look in the eye and barely talk to? There were plenty of students in that review who would have died to get the telephone offer I received. Was I going to be his welfare case, or was I going to be his black bitch?

We met the next day in his conference room lined with books, a lot of them, and almost all monographs on the gods of modernism. There were Corbu's complete works, a rare find, and Mies, including an old Museum of Modern Art monograph on Mies too big and too flimsy to stand up, which was laid out on a shelf like a trophy or an idol, the very same edition that had been stolen from the school's library where photocopies of its cover were displayed on the library's wall with the word "WANTED" printed across the top. Sitting in that conference room was like sitting in a classroom devoted to the great books on modern architecture. I was afraid there was going to be a quiz. There was a model at one end of the conference table. Not bad. Made of white Strathmore board. It was kind of crude when you looked at it close. The walls didn't hit the base quite right. It looked like maybe it was just a study model, but they displayed it like it was ready to be shown otherwise. Why was it sitting here? They hadn't caught on to making models out of bass wood yet. Was I going to be the next generation model maker? Give me a break. That was not my aspiration. But if he was willing to pay well and I could name my hours, it might not be such a bad deal. It wouldn't hurt to add his name to my résumé under work experience. The last architectural job I had was such a flop that it would never make my résumé and would provide no references. Was this going to be a better investment of my time, or should I just keep waiting tables until something better came along? Until I got a degree, nothing better was going to come along. Working for Robert A. Michael would be a plum job.

The reason having outside jurors on your reviews is important is because it is a way to get your work in front of professionals without having to go begging door to door. My fellow comrades would fall all over themselves when someone famous was about to appear. Who got to go first, who got to go last, who got to go in front of whom, etc.? Timing was thought to be everything. Get in front of them before they are bored, cranky, and stupefied by a dozen presentations, or wait until they've seen all the crap your classmates have shown so that they can see real talent emerging at the very end and there is time to take a juror aside and ask if they are hiring.

But there were no overtures after the crit, no "Give me a call; we might be hiring in a few months." No "I really like your work. You show a lot of promise. When you get your portfolio together, let me know," etc., etc. Robert grabbed his coat, said he had a meeting, and took off as though he was happy to get out of there.

Now, two days later, there we were facing each other. The attire you wear for a jury is not what you wear for an interview. After all, you don't want to appear as though you (supposing you are a woman) are going to upset the boys in the back room and slow down productivity with some kind of sexual distraction. I was presentable. I couldn't afford any real "business attire"; you know, the double-breasted suit and the starched button-down shirt but without the tie that made you look kind of like a man. That would have been over the top for this firm anyway. This was not Skidmore, Owings & Merrill. These folks at Robert A. Michael and Associates were kind of a tweedy, khakis-and-blue-denim-shirt kind of crowd. Getting dressed up for them meant getting the silk rep tie out of your tweed jacket pocket and putting on each for the allotted time when you were to look "nice" or professional or whatever. As soon as you hit the back room, off came the coat and tie and the sleeves got rolled up. "Time to do some real work" was what that gesture said. I saw it all the time with faculty. "Come into the studio, loosen the tie, throw off the jacket, roll up the sleeves, and give me that 'move over, sister' look; I'm going to show you how it is done."

So there we were, me in my pressed jeans, loose-fitting sweater, and a bra so I didn't let any erect nipples spoil the interview. I put my portfolio on the table. Robert stared at it and then brushed it aside.

"This is not an interview," he said rather curtly. "I was impressed by your work and your presentation, and I want you to work for me." Who was he hiring? The Black Bitch Nubian Queen who had behaved like a slut or the architectural wannabe who was now humbly sitting across the Corbu table that at this moment served as a conference room artifact? Funny how architects liked to be surrounded by the objects created by their heroes as though some of their genius might rub off if they sat at the table and on the chairs those they considered their mentors had designed. The chairs were by Mies, I noticed, the Bruno chair, and they looked old. They must have been worth a fortune, modern antiques, the originals (he probably bought them secondhand), the real thing when the chrome and leather and the construction were put together in a manner to last longer than the life of their owner, assembled in Czechoslovakia before it was invaded by the Nazis and unlike the knockoffs that now pervaded the market. I loved doing research on these things.

I couldn't imagine Corbu or Mies ever talking to the likes of me across a table in their atelier. They probably didn't use their own furniture, except for a prototype, but to think of them in the other half of the century interviewing a Black Bitch Nubian Queen was all but impossible to imagine. Now Robert had his chance. In the profession of architecture the times were progressing, incrementally.

I never was under confident and wouldn't be considered an underachiever. Daddy took care of that. I was his little Coca. "See what Coca has drawn!" The refrigerator door was always chock-full of sketches Coca had made. Daddy started making portfolios of them after a while. The way I pronounced Coca came out more like KoKo. When I got to architecture school I changed the spelling of my nickname to KoKo. I liked the symmetry. My given name is Cassandra after Cassandra Wilson, the jazz singer. Both Daddy and Mommy loved Cassandra Wilson. I have a sneaking suspicion I was conceived while Cassandra Wilson was working her spell on Daddy and Mommy and that's how I got my name.

I was still Coca when I stopped at a construction site across the street from our apartment. They were building an addition to the school there, and it was the first building activity I had ever seen in our neighborhood of apartment buildings nearly a century old.

I remember standing outside the construction fence to watch the crane work and the men shuffle back and forth and listening to the sounds of hammering and watching the sparks fly when the steel was being welded, marveling at the crane, a big monstrous mechanical dinosaur that could lift anything, even hoppers filled with concrete, which dripped like they were big ladles of soup or molasses.

A black man approached me from the other side of the chain-link fence one day. I had seen him before. He wasn't always there. He would show up about once a week. He was always dressed nicely, in a suit and tie, and he always managed to keep his shiny black shoes from getting dusty or muddy, which the construction site was all the time. This day he walked right over to the fence where I was standing and said, "Hi."

I said, "Hi," back.

"What you doin' here?" he said. I said I was just watching what was going on. He said, "Well, come on in and watch it from inside." He led me through the gate where trucks came and went to a metal building—actually a house trailer where they'd added a little porch and some stairs. Inside there were men drinking coffee, most of them dressed in their construction outfits with tools hanging all over them, with big dirty boots, and they were all big men. It was hard to figure out whether they were white or black or Latino or Asian or what. They all had long hair, some pulled back in ponytails, and some had mustaches and others beards. Their hard hats were pulled down close to their eyes, so it was hard to see their whole face. They all seemed to have dark complexions, even those I knew to be white, because of the sun, I guess.

The man in the suit was an engineer, and he took me over to a table and showed me a stack of drawings several inches thick. I was amazed. "Who made all these drawings?"

"The architect," he said, and he explained that the drawings showed how the building was to be put together. He explained that his job was to make sure the building was put together the way the architect showed. I knew then that I wanted to be an architect. I wanted to be the one to show how the building should be built, what it would look like, how it would work. An architect. That was for me.

When I went home, I told Daddy I wanted to be an architect. "An architect?" he said, with a little question mark at the end. Just a little question mark. More a quizzical upbeat turn to the phrase at its end, like the way Miles would end some of his riffs. "An architect?"

"Yes, Daddy, an architect. They do drawings that make it possible to build things. I want to be one of them."

Then Daddy said, "Well, Coca, I don't think there are any women architects, and I don't think there are any black women architects, but you sure can be the first at whatever you want to do." He would repeat that often when I got discouraged with my studies, and others, many others, told me that I wasn't going to make it in the white man's world of architecture.

Now I was sitting across from Robert A. Michael as a black woman who was nearly an architect. He had asked me there because he knew I was a black woman wanting to be an architect. A black woman who already showed some promise far enough along in her academic career that he was willing to look past the "wannabe" thing and accept me as someone who could do certain tasks that could make a contribution to his firm. No looking at an anonymous résumé and portfolio. No picking up on the name of your black sorority in your résumé under memberships. Résumés looked pretty much the same once you entered the professional program. There was no time for cultural identity stuff. That had to come earlier or not at all. So how do you discover black architects? You hunt them down in their lair. Here I was Robert's catch.

Was I going to be a field slave or a house slave? What did he have in mind for me? Today, here in the "not an interview" situation, Robert seemed comfortable with me. He looked me in the eyes. We shook hands gently, even though his hands were large and his fingers long and strong. We talked awhile. He asked me where I was from, where I lived, how long I'd been in the program. He asked me how I had become interested in architecture, and I told him of the scrapbook of my drawings that Daddy kept and the meeting with the engineer who told me what architects did. I didn't tell him that everyone I talked to said, "*No,* you can't be an architect. You'll never be an architect. You're black, you're a woman, you're not rich, you haven't gone to the right schools, and you'll never know anyone who would ever want to build anything or could build anything. You'll be nothing. Go find yourself an architect man, honey. That way you can at least feel a part of that architect thing you want to do." Shit. The more they talked, the more convinced I became that this was my destiny. I knew it was my destiny.

In the architectural world the beginning architect was often called a nigger. Not so much now that the N word has been eliminated from polite conversation, or at least the vocabulary of the white world. Niggers can still call niggers niggers, but you would never hear that word in an architect's office. Was that word used to describe Wesley Snipes's character Flipper in Spike Lee's movie *Jungle Fever*? I don't remember. Maybe it was used when this "happily married and successful architect" was ceremoniously asked to leave the white majority owner's offices. Get the irony of "majority owners"? Maybe he heard the name *nigger* called behind his back. But the word *nigger* has been replaced with the noun *intern*. He/she is the one to make the coffee, make sure the conference room is clean, the wastebaskets emptied . . . you get the picture.

House slave, field slave? Would Robert know the difference? Probably not. He was a nice northern guy, a liberal guy who was shielded from the harsh realities of life, making it easier to believe in what he believed. If asked, he would certainly say that he was against slavery, wondering why he would even be asked the question.

"Follow me," Robert said. We walked through the studio together, Robert in front. He was enough larger than me and the aisle between the drafting tables narrow enough that I was hidden behind him as we walked. We stopped at the first semi-cubicle. Robert turned and said, "I'd like you to meet KoKo Wilson. I am hoping she will join our office. KoKo, this is . . ." and he would mumble a name. This occurred several times as we marched the length of the office. Every time the reaction was the same. Eyes would get this startled look at first. Then this all-male cast would glance at Robert as if to say, "Did you not notice that this is a woman; did you not notice that this woman is black?" And before Robert could feel compelled to answer this unspoken question, he would move on to the next desk. The younger guys seemed less surprised. Perhaps the very youngest among them had seen me in school. I stood out. I didn't see anyone my daddy's age, someone in their late forties or early fifties. It was like that age group had been nuked.

PRESENTATION

The Intern

Robert told me he was surprised to be asked to interview for the job. The firm Robert A. Michael and Associates, Architects, was well known for its award-winning churches; that was for sure. That would be an obvious reason for interviewing Robert. We learned there were just two other firms on the interview list: Rawlings and Rawlings and Associates, Inc., an African American firm that did mostly post offices and warehouses for the government and had no track record doing churches; and a cousin of one of the building committee members who was just starting his own firm after graduating from Harvard earlier in the year.

I learned of the interview one day when Robert came by my desk to inspect the model I was working on for the Amy and Andy House. After looking at the model for a moment he said, "How would you like to go to a job interview with me on Saturday morning?" One of those rhetorical questions.

"Me? Why me?"

"Well," said Robert, "I just thought you would like to see how an interview works and since this is an interview for Reverend Ike's church expansion (knowing that I would know who Reverend Ike was), I thought you might know someone there." Now Reverend Ike was almost a household name in the black community, but I hadn't ever been in his church, hadn't even been past it. I hadn't been in a church since I started going to architecture school. When were you going to do church with all the other stuff you were doing, especially if you were trying to hold down a job too, and how would I find time to go to this interview on Saturday morning? Then Robert piped up: "Oh, don't worry; this will count as part of your hours. I'll pay you." *Damn right,* I said to myself. Robert continued, "Interviews are one of the most important things architects do these days. Gone are the days when you can get a job because you are somebody's cousin."

I came in Friday night to help Robert put together a presentation for the interview. He was allowed twenty minutes for a presentation and ten minutes for questions and answers, about the same amount of time for a school crit. We had to be at the church at 9:00 a.m., a challenge for me, who like my classmates likes to work late and sleep late. Robert pulled some slides out of the slide file and put them on the light table. He shuffled them around and then asked me to look for the boards he had used for the interview a few weeks earlier for the St. Matthew

Methodist Church commission. He was still waiting to hear from them. He was one of ten firms they had interviewed, and they were going to make a short list of three to interview again. He was hoping to make the short list.

I found the boards, four thirty-by-forty-inch boards that had mounted on them enlarged photographs, some color and some black-and-white, of churches Robert had designed and built. There were also reproductions of sketches and freehand plans blown up larger than their original size to make them look more impressive. There were also a few newspaper and magazine clippings that had also been copied and enlarged featuring Robert A. Michael's awards for church architecture. But there was a problem. Along the bottom of the boards ran the words "St. Matthew Methodist Church, Robert A. Michael and Associates, Architects." The title block was intentionally subliminal. It associated the two names—St. Matthew Methodist Church and Robert A. Michael—across each of the four presentation boards. The articles that featured previous awards were to indicate that St. Matthews would also get an award-winning design, and hiring an award-winning architect would help them raise money for their edifice. I learned from Robert that to raise money you first had to raise expectations, raise hopes, and create a vision. The architect had a key role to play in that part of the endeavor.

When I pointed out the confusing title block, Robert said, "Just print up a new one and paste it over the St. Matthews title block. They won't know the difference, and I've already got my spiel down for that; in fact, I'll use the same slide show." I was curious. Was Robert's presentation for every church job the same? He had shown me the invitation for the interview. They were interviewing just three firms, the invitation confirmed. The job was advertised as an addition to the facilities of the AME church at the corner of First and Maple Streets. It went on to explain the success of the church's before—and after-school programs, the food and shelter program for the homeless, the programs for the elderly, the need for a choir practice room, more space indoors and outdoors for its youth athletic programs, etc. It didn't say anything about a new sanctuary, but the St. Matthews presentation only addressed Robert's design of sanctuaries. All the photos were of new churches and their sanctuaries. There were no photos of classrooms, offices, and gyms, just sanctuaries. I wanted to bring that to Robert's attention, but he seemed unfazed by the disconnect between what was to be his presentation and the request for a proposal he received from Reverend Isaac Donnelee.

It didn't take long to put together the presentation once Robert decided to use everything from the St. Matthews presentation. Robert departed, saying, "Bring the boards, the easels, the slides, and projector and I'll see you at the church at 8:45 a.m. We don't want to be late. I lost a job once because I was five minutes late for an interview. I'll never forget it. Lesson learned. Better shoot for 8:30. Know where it is? I'll see you there," and then as he was about to close the door, he continued, "Thanks for doing this for me. Dress nice, will you? Know what I mean?"

Now I was left with the decision of trying to pack all this shit in my car that night or come in early next morning to pick it up and cart it to the meeting on the Southside. To be safe I would have to allow another half hour or so though traffic that early on a Saturday morning shouldn't be too bad. I would have to get up by 6:00 a.m. so I could "dress nice." Who the hell could dress nice at 6:00 a.m.? I could pile all this shit in my car right then, but it would sure as hell get ripped off where I live. The lock on my car was broken anyway, and I wasn't about to drag all this stuff up to my apartment and then back down again. *Shit,* I said to myself. I didn't even know if I could get thirty-by-forty boards into my little beat-up Civic even with the back seat down. Then what? Why did Robert just assume I could bring all this shit? He'd never seen my car. I suppose he thought I drove a Cadillac. You couldn't get but two people in his Porsche, and it seemed that he planned it that way. His gophers (can't call them niggers anymore) were employed to do all his trucking. But let's face it. Tomorrow he would have his nigger doing what niggers do.

I woke up with this resentful feeling. I didn't have much of a choice except to go to this interview. I knew there was more to it than "letting me see how an interview works." This was an African American church, and I was an African American Black Bitch Nubian Queen Architect Wannabe "associate." Associate didn't really mean anything in Robert's firm. There were no real associates—that is, someone other than Robert who had a financial stake in the firm. No, Robert would tell us we were all associates, all equal, and he thought of himself as an associate too. We were collectively, after all, Robert A. Michael and Associates,

Architects. But there was just one Robert A. Michael, that person who was more equal than all the others who were called associates.

So there I was climbing the stairs to the office at this ungodly hour on Saturday morning. I prayed that I could get all the stuff in my car. It took three trips down the elevator, and I was afraid to put anything in the car until I could get everything in the lobby because I couldn't lock the car and didn't want anything to get ripped off while I was hustling back and forth from the studio to the elevator to the car and back again. But the lobby was just as insecure as my car. I put all the stuff behind one of the dusty delphinium plants that was supposed to be maintained, along with all the others by a landscape service that consisted of a bunch of goons who didn't even have a clue as to the names of these plants or give a rat's ass as to whether they lived or died. The "service" was just paid to give the plants some water, pick up the dead leaves, and dust them with a feather duster, which was an action more akin to passing a magic wand over the plant and saying a few holy words in the hope the plant would live or die, but if it were to die, it should go quickly so there would be less need to pick up dead leaves. The dead leaves crunched beneath my knock-off Kate Spade pumps, and more fell as I propped the boards behind the plastic tub that held the plants as I scurried off to get the projector. The boards would be of no interest to a passing kleptomaniac, but the projector surely would. I prayed that the boards would fit in the back of my beat-up Civic and that I could close the hatchback door. They did, just barely. The easels were piled into the front (reminder to suggest to Robert he get some folding easels), and the projector sat on the floor. Then I remembered that I had forgotten the slide trays. Oh shit, the slide trays. Two guys were cruising down the street on their skateboards taking it all in. I couldn't tell if they were interested in me or the stuff in the car. I let them pass and turn the corner, and then I beat it back to the elevator, one eye on the car, the other on the indicator, hoping those guys wouldn't come back. What were people doing on the street at eight in the morning anyway? Hoodlums, vagrants, gang bangers, leftovers from the night before? Eight in the morning? *How did it get to be so late?* I thought. *Jesus, I've got to hurry. Is the fucking elevator stuck or what?* In this kind of situation everything takes longer. For me, the elevator took longer to arrive. It took longer to get to the fourth floor. It took me longer to find the key and get it in the lock. It took me longer to get to the other end of the office and to get the slide tray where I had left it on my desk. And all the time I saw these guys who'd heard the car door slam rather than the engine whirring and the car taking off and got it figured out that I had to go back in the office for something and this was their opportunity to loot my car. Someone had called the elevator back to the first floor. I couldn't wait. I took the stairs. Two at a time. This is where it helps to have long legs, but it was tough in my "look nice" shoes. Fortunately I wore the look nice slacks rather than the look nice skirt. The skirt made me take baby steps, but it showed my ass real nice and it was good for a lot of things. But reason told me, even at 6:00 a.m., that this was a church interview and I didn't need to wear—shouldn't wear—my short skirt.

The guys were there, looking my car up and down. They sure wouldn't want to steal the car, and I wasn't in it, so it must be the stuff. But they had a puzzled look on their faces as if to say, "We could steal it, but what would we do with it?" They saw me and looking my way real cool like said, "Can we help you, lady?" Our ages weren't that much different, but wearing high heels I knew made me a lady. "Can we help you, lady?" They were looking me up and down, and not in the way you would look at a lady.

"No thanks, guys," I said, and I was out of there.

I found the church. It was pretty easy because Robert was standing outside pacing back and forth with his Porsche parked across the street and a not-so-tough-looking teenager, actually he was kind of wimpy looking except if you were a white guy afraid of the hood, sitting on the stoop behind it staring at its silverness. "Don't worry," Robert said. "I've paid him to watch it. He'll watch yours too. Where have you been? I've been here twenty-five minutes. We'll be late."

"Where's the entrance?" I said as we both hauled the stuff out of my car.

"I don't know," he said as though it were an insult that I would expect him to know where the entrance was. *What the fuck was he doing for the twenty-five minutes he was waiting for me?* I wondered. We were standing in front of the sanctuary, which would not be the front door into the office. Robert indicated that he'd already tried the sanctuary door and found it locked. Along the chain-link fence that closed off the churchyard, there was a gate that was standing ajar as though someone had opened it for us. We headed there. I had already begun asking myself how one could make something an award winner here, in this beat-up neighborhood among all this architectural flotsam and jetsam that perhaps one day had been a very nice but modest church.

A door closest to the sanctuary seemed most promising as we both mentally read the plan of the building and figured that would be where the offices should be located. We were right. The door opened onto a dingy hallway. On the wall opposite was a piece of paper pulled from a ring binder with the word "INTERVIEW" scrawled on it and an arrow pointing down the hall. We proceeded in the direction of the arrow. The hall opened onto an alcove, and there we encountered the other interviewees. Two guys from Rawlings and Rawlings introduced themselves, but neither was a Rawling. Both were black; one guy was little and the other big, so big he looked like he would be more comfortable in a football uniform. But both of them were dressed nicely, not overdressed for a Saturday morning. They both had two-button dark brown suits, nicely tailored with pleated pants with a nice break over their well-polished wingtips and tan button-down shirts buttoned all the way to their chins but no tie. They looked as though they were dressed the same, but then again they weren't. The difference in their size would make them look different anyway. They looked to be in their late thirties or early forties, and both wore wedding rings.

Another guy sitting on the only chair in the little cubbyhole of the waiting area/vestibule must have been the recent export from Harvard. He was in his late twenties or early thirties and was thin and tall, almost emaciated looking, and white. Very white. A real pale male. He got up, shook hands, and then sat down real fast as though he didn't want to lose his seat. It appeared that he didn't like this early morning hour any better than we did. The two black married guys probably had kids and got up at this hour anyway, but I could see a comrade in the Harvard guy. He looked not quite awake and as though he had difficulty getting his clothes on or hadn't taken them off from the night before. He had that studied Bohemian look, with that two-day growth of beard that could signify so many things, from trying to grow a beard to not caring to having better things to do than shave to attempting to look like any one of a trillion male celebrities seen in ads for a men's cologne. He wore black denim pants, a black T-shirt, and a black three-button sport coat without a vent. He didn't appear to have anything with him, and then I noticed the standard architectural intern portfolio, black imitation leather ring binder, cradled between a leg of his chair and his own leg.

The crew from Rawlings and Rawlings had boards wrapped in brown paper. So there we were: the Rawlings crew all wrapped in brown, Mr. Harvard Graduate School of Design dressed in New York basic architectural black and Robert and me. Robert had on a tweed jacket, khaki pants, a white button-down shirt, a rep tie, and penny loafers. I was an incongruous match. I stood an inch taller than Robert in my Kate Spade knockoffs. Black shoes, tan slacks, darker than khaki, and my red blouse. Red, why had I picked my red blouse? I chose not to wear one with a loose neck or one that was too tight fitting; yet I wanted one that would get people's attention. Why? Red would do it. Red it was. Flaming red. Bauhaus *red.* For Robert there were only three colors, black, white, and red, and sometimes gray. I knew he would approve.

THE NEW ZEITGEIST

The Associate

Shortly after Robert and I arrived in the crowded alcove, a large middle-aged black nicely dressed woman appeared. The kind of woman who could be an advertisement in the Sunday magazine fashion section illustrating how to dress for success even if you are a size twenty. Given her upscale fashionable wardrobe, it seemed apparent that she was one of the interviewers and not one of the church staff. She introduced herself as Eta Mae Smith, chairwoman of the building committee. The interviews would be conducted in the order in which people had arrived, she explained, which meant that Rawlings and Rawlings would go first, then the Harvard guy whose name we hadn't caught, and then us. Robert let out an audible sigh. Eta Mae explained that the interviews would be for a half hour, no more. We would have twenty minutes to present, and there would be a ten-minute question period from the committee. We would be notified on Monday of the committee's decision. The interviews would start in another ten or fifteen minutes; they were still waiting for some other committee members to arrive. It was already 9:15 by now. Robert emitted another noticeable sigh.

"Excuse us," Robert said to Eta Mae Smith, "but since we are last, we would like to go out to get a cup of coffee."

"Fine," she said. "But we have coffee right here."

"We have some things to discuss," Robert replied. "We'll be back in plenty of time for our interview."

"Don't be late," she said. "These people have other things to do. It was difficult enough to get them out here on a Saturday morning. They won't want to wait." Robert assured her we would be back in less than forty-five minutes. "Oh, and by the way," Eta Mae called after us, "you can take the projector with you. We have one of our own for you to use." I had noticed that neither of the other two interviewees had projectors. They must have asked. Of all the times Robert had been to an interview, why hadn't he asked if they had a projector?

He said, "Do you mind if we keep this here just in case?"

"No, not at all," Eta Mae replied with a certain disdain in her voice, as if to say, "You don't think our projector is going to be good enough for you?"

The Harvard guy was still sitting in the alcove fidgeting with his portfolio when we returned. It was evident that Rawlings and Rawlings were still being interviewed, and it was nearly an hour later. I could hear Robert say, "Fuck," under his breath. "There goes my tennis match. I'd better call. Excuse me." Robert didn't like carrying a cell phone around. He hated the cell phone but kept one in his car. That was where he was headed. He had no sooner left than the Rawlings and Rawlings guys appeared with smiles on their faces. Eta Mae said, "Thank you, gentlemen, very much. We'll look forward to seeing you again." Did that mean they had already made their decision? "Please, Mr. Harvard GSD (I missed the name again), would you join us now?" And she and Mr. Whatisname left.

The Rawlings big guy and little guy looked at me, and the smiles left their faces and turned into grins. Then the little guy said, "You've got this job wrapped up. They want someone who's designed churches, someone with a track record, someone who can help them raise money. They interviewed us anticipating the pushback they would get if they didn't interview a minority firm. But this was a great interview for us." *Why?* I thought. "There's a developer in there who's gonna build an office building and wants to talk with us. What a break. You never know when those things will happen. This Harvard guy is a friend of a friend. You know how that works?" *Thanks for the compliment,* I thought.

"You know how that works?" *Well, no. I'm at the bottom of the learning curve here.*

"How'd you get a job with this Michael's guy anyway?" the little guy asked. They didn't wait for an answer. That question took balls.

Mr. Harvard GSD came out of the room with Eta Mae just as Robert entered the hall from the opposite end. The second interview hadn't taken much more than fifteen minutes. Lucky Robert was back. Mr. Harvard GSD had his portfolio under his arm and his head hung low. It wasn't difficult to see this had not gone well for him despite the fact that he had a relative somewhere in that room. *Not much different from a crit at school,* I thought. Are the hazing's you get during reviews at school just a way of preparing us for rejection during client interviews when we become professionals?

Getting the first job on your own is always the most difficult, we are told in school. That's why you've got to work for someone else for a while. Develop a body of work that you can identify with even if it's done in someone else's firm. Architecture is an old man's game. Even in this age of political correctness, people still say that. If you want to be discovered as a child genius, you are better off trying to develop a tech startup. Even with all the child millionaires who now should make up a huge client base for young architects, they still say get some gray hair and a paunch and you become one with your client. Of course this doesn't apply to Black Bitch Nubian Queen Architect Wannabes.

Eta Mae said, "Would you please bring your projector with you? Our bulb seems to have burned out." Robert was savvier than I had given him credit for. Obviously he'd been in this situation before. The room was small, and there were more than a dozen people in it, sitting two rows deep on metal folding chairs, behind metal folding tables that are ubiquitous to any institutional meeting room. In the front was a small collapsible screen on a tripod that made the screen slightly askew so that the top and bottom were not parallel to the floor. Robert hated misalignments. He claimed total distraction when things, architectural things, weren't perfect, and how could he show his slides on a screen that was so askew with the room in which it sat? He busied himself with wedging paper under one of the three legs as he tried to get the screen parallel to the room's geometry. The ceiling of the room was eight feet high, maybe less. The projector was on a stand at the back of the room. I had to set up easels and put the boards on them, and there was barely room on either side of the screen for two easels. Robert was still fidgeting with the screen. There was hardly a place to put the other projector and to get ours in place, but I managed. Robert was now finished with the screen and trying to find a place to stand so he was in front of neither the screen nor the presentation boards. By this time the committee was a little fidgety. Some of them had been there for nearly two hours without a break, and they'd all had coffee by the looks of the Styrofoam cups lining the edge of the fold-up metal tables. A silent anthem raised by the "jury" to the heavens was heard saying, "Let's get this over with."

Robert was presented to the committee by Eta Mae, who said, "I am pleased to introduce Robert A. Michael of Robert A. Michael, Architect." The way she said it made it sound like this was a very small firm composed of Robert A. Michael as she dropped the Associates. "Robert A. Michael and Associates!" I wanted to scream. And here I am associate of the day. Eta Mae concluded the introduction, "Mr. Michael, the floor is yours." The building committee was about half black and half white. Reverend Ike sat in the front middle. His picture was frequently in the papers when the paper needed a feel-good news moment. He wasn't difficult to recognize. He had a way of dressing that made him look like a man of the cloth. All black attire. But not the same kind of black outfit the Harvard guy wore. The trousers were bought off the rack but were nicely pleated and well pressed. The shirt was black, buttoned all the way to the chin, and it too was nicely pressed with a little starch in it. The shoes were black with plain toes, and he wore a plain black leather belt. Everything was plain but neat and tidy. Even his hair, curly nappy hair, was black with just a few highlights of gray complementing his stainless-steel belt buckle and wristwatch, the only things that weren't black.

The other committee members were an assortment of black and white stereotypes. The blacks all seemed like parishioners, right at home here. The whites represented some other tribe, obviously not so at home here. Mothers, sisters, daughters, fathers, brothers, secretaries, vice presidents, construction managers, bankers, lawyer, real estate folks, and others of the cloth. It was hard to tell who was who, but I sensed that they all had been carefully chosen for the constituency they represented. Eta Mae didn't introduce any of them, and I could see that Robert was desperately trying to size up his audience. Who was this motley crew? But he did recognize Reverend Ike and astutely stepped forward to shake his hand.

Robert began, "Pastor Donnelee"—using Reverend Ike's last name—"and committee members, it is a pleasure to be with you today. I want to thank you for the opportunity to be interviewed for the important task that lies ahead of you. But before I begin, I would like to introduce you to my associate and colleague, Cassandra Wilson." Whenever people use my God-given name, it gets the jerk of the head as though people are expecting to see the "real" Cassandra Wilson. I can never figure out whether people are disappointed or not. There is always a quizzical look on faces. Even for those who are not jazz aficionados, there seems to be a glimmer of recognition that goes with the name. But then they soon discover that this is an impersonator in their midst. "KoKo, would you please come up here," he said, motioning for me to leave the projector and join him.

"I want to tell you how fortunate I am to have KoKo as an associate," Robert continued. Associate? The first time I was "officially" called an associate. I thought to myself, *Congratulations on the promotion, KoKo. Is that* associate *spelled with a small a or a capital A?* I was trying to listen to Robert at the same time moving to get around the tables without offending anyone by putting my behind in their face and wondering what I would say in the event Robert asked me to say something. "Ms. Wilson is a very promising architectural student at the university here, in her fifth year. I met her while visiting the school for a review of student work, and I immediately recognized her immense talent and asked her to work for me. She flattered me by saying yes. I want you to know that a census of architects conducted recently revealed that there were only 1,060 registered African American architects in the United States. That is only 1 percent of all the registered architects in the United States. And, of those only ninety are African American women. Less than one tenth of 1 percent of all architects practicing in the United States are African American women, and I am fortunate to have a woman who wants to join that illustrious group as one of my associates. She will be working with me side by side on this project, and I am anxious for you to get to know her." Robert's agenda was now fully revealed. I was trotted to the front of the room to make sure that everyone saw I was an African American woman, a black woman. I wanted to clarify that by saying so everyone could hear, "I am the Black Bitch Nubian Queen Architect Wannabe who is looking forward to jamming with you all." But I didn't.

Robert was now ready for the presentation. "I am going to show some slides of our work. I have brought along boards that illustrate other examples, and if there is time at the end of the interview, I would like you to come forward and I can tell you a little more about each of these *award-winning* churches." Somehow *award-winning* stood out in this sentence. Robert took a little longer saying this word. He said it a little louder, a little more in the affirmative, and somehow if you didn't get anything else he had said, "*award-winning churches*" got lodged in your cranium. Eta Mae turned the lights out and I turned the projector on, and it was totally black for a scary instant until the screen was filled with an upside-down image of a church. Oh my God. What a way to start. But Robert wasn't flustered at all. "Excuse us," he said (nice to implicate himself). "These are new slides that I've had made for this interview, and some may have been mounted improperly." *What bullshit,* I thought. If anyone looked at these slides, they could see they'd been used plenty of times before, and I was just hopeful that the fingerprints on them didn't obscure the image. Let us pray together that this is the only slide that is upside down. It was.

Robert tended to ramble. He would get very excited seeing his own work on the screen in front of him. He would talk about how the light would enter a window and touch the altar. He would describe in detail the design of the organ and altar furniture and the pews that he secretly enjoyed designing as much as the sanctuary. He described how the sanctuary would be used for processions (marriage, baptisms, and funerals), where the choir stood, how the minister and choir entered the sanctuary, the acoustics, and the light again, and the furniture again. The slides would begin to repeat themselves. They were fundamentally the same sequence for each of the six "award-winning" projects. First the site plan and orientation, the direction of the sun, where parishioners would park their cars, and how they arrived at the door of the sanctuary. Then a plan of the sanctuary, where the windows were (light again), the organization of the space from the mundane of where people hung their coats and where the minister stood to shake hands with the departing congregation to the proportions of the plan. Robert always based his plans on some kind of geometrical proportioning system that for him was as close as any earthly mortal might get to creating something that might please the gods. Robert, if pushed, confessed to being a Unitarian, but he never went to church and as far as anyone knew never gave to a church either.

Robert took too long with the plans. For most audiences it was difficult to understand a plan. Things went better when they were able to see photos. There was a sameness to the photos of the church interiors, however. I tried to see this presentation from the eyes of the committee, and I was all of a sudden embarrassed by the fact Robert's presentation focused on church sanctuary's exclusively and this job was about an addition to the church to better serve community functions. It was also painfully obvious that all the churches Robert showed were freestanding buildings out in a field somewhere, not houses of worship in some inner-city urban confinement. I was hoping that Robert would somehow make a connection to the program at hand. He didn't. *Please let the presentation end quickly so the committee will not be aware of what I am aware of,* I said to myself.

Robert finished and asked for the lights to come on. He motioned me to the front of the room that had no space for me and asked, "Do you have any questions for us?"

Reverend Ike was the first to speak up. "You realize, don't you, Mr. Michael, that we are planning to build community facilities here, not a sanctuary?"

"Oh yes," Robert replied. "I understand fully. Those same qualities of religious expression can be built into any ecclesiastical setting, Reverend Ike. I try to imbue my religious buildings with a sense of God, no matter how humble their utilization might be."

"We don't think of our work in any hierarchical way, Mr. Michael," Reverend Ike replied. "We think a basketball court can be as important a place for doing God's work as a sanctuary or a chapel. I hope you understand that. Our budget for this project is going to be the budget one might have for a school or office building. We are talking concrete block and vinyl tile here, Mr. Michael. Do you think you can do an award-winning project for us using a humble program, humble materials, and a humble budget?"

"God is in the details," Robert replied, perhaps too glibly using what had become a cliché even outside of the architect's narrow world. "We will give you a beautiful facility. One you can be proud of."

The committee was clearly getting fidgety. The weariness of participating in more than two hours of listening and being talked to was taking its toll, that along with the couple of cups of coffee that everyone had now helped move them toward the door simultaneously. Of course everyone could not get out at once. The Reverend Ike was lodged between a table, and Robert with no place to go, giving the Reverend the opportunity to ask a question he apparently didn't want to ask in front of everyone. I don't think he wanted me to hear it either. But I was intent on hearing how this interview might proceed now that it was one on one. Reverend Ike said, slightly under his breath, "This African American woman you have hired is going to be working on this project, is she not?"

"Oh yes," said Robert. "She will be my associate on this project. She will be the junior member of the team, as it were, but we'll be co-equals."

"Good," said Reverend Ike. "I think she could make a great difference in the success of this project." Robert gave me a wink when he saw that I had overheard their conversation.

CONFLICTING ASPIRATIONS

The Convert

It didn't sound like the typical male invitation: "Come up to my place this Saturday night. We're having a party"—to find you were the only invitee and *you* were going to be the party. Robert's invitation seemed innocent enough. When we left the interview and were headed for our cars, Robert asked me what I was doing for lunch. I said I had to get ready for a structures exam on Monday. Robert didn't seem to hear me and said, "Why don't you come to my place for lunch?" He said it as a statement, not a question.

"Well, I . . ."

"Please," Robert said, "I'd like to talk to you about the interview and get to know you better. And I really want to show you my house. It says everything I have to say about architecture."

Okay," I said reluctantly, thinking there goes the afternoon. I had just been given a lesson in Robert's ecclesiastical architecture and now we were going to move on to the lesson in domestic architecture. We agreed that I would follow Robert's lead. He promised to go slow, but slow for Robert's Porsche was about as fast as my CRX would go since it had needed a tune-up really badly for better than a year. We headed north away from the Southside, and I realized that I didn't have a clue where Robert lived despite seeing his house published and the awards it had received mounted on the reception area walls opposite Ms. Jones's in the office of Robert A. Michael and Associates, Architects.

After we left the city, we began driving along the bluffs above Lake Michigan. My car noticed the pull of gravity as we would climb and descend the hills and valleys created by these enormous dunes even as Robert's Porsche appeared as though it wanted to take wing around every curve and at the top of every hill. Even when the Porsche disappeared from view, I could hear Robert shifting down to take the next curve and then the roar of the engine as he got into the curve and accelerated as though being fired from a slingshot aimed toward the next opportunity for acceleration. This answered the question of the Porsche. Robert seemed to be having a ball, just as he must every day as he went up and down this topography flexing his macho motoring skills.

From around one corner I saw the house perched several stories above on a promontory with steep drops on either side. This was the iconic view. Unlike the iconic view of Wright's Falling Water, which one couldn't see except by hopping across the creek called Bear Run, this view of Robert's house was accessible to anyone who dared stop on this winding road with poor visibility. I could think only of the courage it took the photographer to get this shot, at the right time of day with the sun setting beyond the house, the camera propped on a tripod in the middle of the road with the photographer hoping there would be no approaching cars. Or did he get permission to block off the road for the hour it would take to get this shot, or have a helper or two helpers, one uphill and one down, flagging down traffic so the shot could be made? And now a lot of foliage had grown up to block this perfect view, but still it was the view by which everyone recognized the Robert A. Michael award-winning house.

Built in the late sixties, the house was still recognized for its contribution to what historians now call mid-century modernism. The house had recently been used as the site for a fashion shoot for *Elle.* As we passed one trophy house after another, I became very self-conscious of the beater I was driving. Might someone take a shot at me thinking I was some ghetto kid stalking Robert for a shakedown or a wholesale house robbery? I forgot that I had my dress-up clothes on. Even a crazy nigger wouldn't go stalking or house robbing in a drop-dead red silk blouse like I had on. I realized that the outfit did not match the car I was driving and was equally relieved thinking that I wouldn't be taken for a maid.

Two simple concrete columns framed an iron gate made of quarter-inch bar stock welded into a two-by-two-inch grid and painted black. The concrete columns had weathered to the color of the rock around them, slightly stained, but otherwise the design of this gate was as modern today as the day it was built, years earlier. The gate swung open as Robert pressed the remote without coming to a full stop, and he had the timing just right as the Porsche followed the swing of the gate without the brake lights going on, Robert shifting down again with the Porsche making a gurgling sound as though it were being strangled, like a dog on a leash as the owner tried to gain control of the beast. The Porsche had been there before and couldn't wait for the next climb.

I hesitated, not knowing whether or not I would get caught in the claws of the mammoth gate, but Robert stuck his hand out the window and motioned for me to come ahead. There was still another story to climb over a gravel path now decidedly narrower. I realized that this was built to driveway specs and not roadway specs, and there was no guardrail as there had been on the highway with its hairpin turns.

While the Porsche might fly if it went over the edge, I knew the Civic would be heavier than a rock, and then I realized that I still had all the stuff from the interview in the car. *Shit,* I said to myself . . . *I still have to take this back to the office and dump it once we are through with lunch and whatever else Robert has in mind.*

I had become very cynical. Beauty has its price, and one of the prices is the come-on, the constant come-on, from black males, white males, white females, and even an occasional black female. I feel like I've lived a sheltered life thanks to Mom and Dad's efforts, but I was never at a party or bar where I haven't been propositioned even when I try to get the "Black Bitch" to dominate the "Nubian Queen." As the gate closed behind us, I realized that I was imprisoned. Robert had explained that this was a good time to show the house because his wife was in New York "shopping." *Does Robert play this routine every Saturday afternoon when his wife is in New York "shopping"?* I wondered to myself.

Robert parked his car outside the garage and motioned for me to do the same. The garage turned away from the house and was matched by a separate identical building that framed a view of the house. I presumed that the symmetrical building housed a boat, gardening stuff, and all the things most people keep in their garages. I wondered if Robert had more stuff in his garage, but no. Robert's garage probably had carpeting, a built-in vac, and maybe even a bidet for his autoerotic desire, the Porsche.

This view of the house had also been captured in an iconic photo. In this photo the house seemed to float above the ground while the horizon appeared to divide the house neatly in half, and the transparency of the house allowed one to see the horizon line change only in hue as it continued through the house and out the other side. *How did Robert achieve this act of levitation?* I asked myself just as Robert asked me, "What do you think?"

A thousand answers raced through my head, and I knew that there was only one that was appropriate: "Wow." But I didn't use this one right away, thinking that was not terribly original and wondering how many times Robert had asked that question, still not tiring of asking it, and how many answers he had gotten back and whether or not he had listened to or remembered any of them.

But in addition to "What do you think?"—obviously about the Robert A. Michael House, the site, the experience—I was "what do you thinking" about the situation. The city seemed miles away; everything I had always associated with was miles away, in another time zone, another century, another epoch; and the one material thing I had besides my clothes—my car, which seemed to be one avenue of escape if needed—now seemed very far away. Why did I begin to feel this sense of panic? I was in this strange place, this architectural place, the kind of place I had only known through pictures, a place that someday might be in the history books for students to study who were interested in exploring the many branches of modernism that emerged after the original modernists, Wright, Corbu, Mies, and the rest of the pantheon of white males.

I also knew, in a more lucid moment, that this was the home of a white guy of flesh and blood who had conceived and built this place and imbued it with a sensuality that had made it famous and had seduced fashion photographers and their models, and still did.

Robert stood in the front doorway in silhouette. He was like one of those little sketch figures architects use in drawings to illustrate the scale of a building. Corb's were the most famous, a figure of a man modeled after the regulation height of a London Bobby, but with bulbous cartoonish calves, thighs, forearms, and biceps, broad shoulders, and a slender waist with the left arm upraised. Corbu used this "modular man" to illustrate an idea he had developed for a proportioning system derived from an ideal man's physical proportions just as Leonardo da Vinci and countless other Renaissance artists had explored the same idea. Harvard graduates still used the Corbu "modular man" to codify their drawings. It was akin to a dog pissing to mark its territory. Robert would never think of using the Corb modular man. He had devised his own, somewhat chunkier, with a broad chest and shoulders but without such contorted limbs and too narrow waistline. Now Robert stood in the doorway like his own "Mikey," as the office crew dubbed the semi-abstract figures Robert would sometimes use in his sketches.

It was easy to see why Robert positioned himself here. Another ritual, I am certain, for first-time visitors. His navel, or where his navel would be, around his belt buckle, was even with the horizon line, which one could see cutting through the all-but-transparent house. Robert had left his jacket in the Porsche so as to not spoil the affect. The door was twice as high as it was wide, creating a double square. But it wasn't the usual 6'8" that doors usually are. It was a few inches shorter, 6'4" perhaps, making the opening shorter but wider, 3'2", than what one would expect. This also made Robert seem taller and slimmer. The effect was outstanding. What would be an ordinary door was transformed into a piece of geometry that beckoned one to figure out other mysteries the house might hold. Its master now standing in the doorway like a midway carny might be beckoning the crowd to come inside to see the naked lady with a beard.

My heart began beating faster, not knowing what to expect next. As I approached the door with Robert still in it, I didn't think he would move. But then as I took the two broad stairs that carried me from the earth to this celestial cloud of a house, Robert stepped back to expose that part of the horizon his body had kept hidden. Furniture, countertops, paintings, railings, everything in the house seemed to pay homage to the dominating line that separated water and sky, and the background became the foreground as in a painting whose central focus was the horizon.

The exterior walls were all glass, floor to ceiling, without a trace of blinds or curtains. The floor and ceiling by contrast were dark, until Robert touched a switch that brought the walls to life. Their painted surface shimmered. Smooth as silk, a milky white. The black slate floor showed highlights from the concealed spots that perfectly illuminated pictures and the wall. The furniture was chrome and black leather. Glass shelves seemed, like the house itself, to float, holding books and small sculptures and various things that begged for closer inspection. The space we were standing in was one big room, but its transparent boundaries made it difficult to judge its true size. The mullions that held the glass in place were so thin that it appeared that the ceiling and floor were separated by a magnetic force field, the kind one might expect to see in a science fiction movie. Four thin round columns, painted a starker white than the walls and hardly noticeable, held the ceiling aloft.

Again, Robert said, "What do you think?" I hadn't answered the last "what do you think?" My emotions were going at a much more rapid clip than either my mind or lips could keep up with. Now it would seem appropriate to say, "Wow." Nothing else came to mind that would be politically correct.

"Would you imagine this house is nearly thirty years old?" A rhetorical question that didn't need an answer. But the question threw the house in another light. Robert was still searching for his place in history. The house surely owed something to Mies's Farnsworth House in Plano, Illinois, which was raised on five-foot stilts to keep it above the floods of the Fox River, which the enhanced elevation didn't do very well. Mies and his client, Dr. Edith Farnsworth, had a legendary battle between them, but the house, once completed in 1951, immediately became a monument to modernism despite its turbulent parentage. Philip Johnson's Glass House was completed in 1949. Both houses had been exhibited in model form in 1947 at the Museum of Modern Art, where Johnson served as a curator. They might be considered twins in the annals of modern architecture. Why do I know this? It's from research I did for a paper on twentieth-century architecture. Robert inherited the ideas of transparency, lightness, geometry, and exposed structure from this era slightly before his time, as it were. He was careful to avoid being caught up in postmodernism, new urbanism, deconstruction, and other movements without names that had marked the years since he conceived this house and others like it.

"I wanted to build a timeless house that spoke to the twentieth century, and I guess I did if they are still asking me to use the house for fashion shoots." Robert was referring to the spread in the magazine *Elle* that had used the house to display a designer's new fall wardrobe collection nearly a year ago. "They were here just a few months ago to do the shoot." I didn't correct him. "They made me get out, put me downtown at the Windham for two days. I was surprised when I saw the pictures to see that they had changed all the furniture. They didn't have to do that. We bought all this furniture with this house in mind. Everything was new. The Corbu LC3, the Noguchi coffee table, the Eames potato chip chairs. We've had to replace some of them, but they are a part of the house. They said they might move the furniture around, but I never thought they'd bring in their own furniture. I didn't know what to think, though it looked pretty good. Mostly stuff from B&B Italia. I wonder if they were connected with the shoot somehow. Never thought of that." Robert didn't realize that it was his furniture that made the house feel less timeless than he had imagined. I am sure in the minds of the young editors of *Elle* he was thought to have a fine collection of modern antiques.

It was a bit confusing as my mind tried to reconcile the tear sheets of photos from *Elle* that were framed and hanging in the reception area of the studio and the reality of the modern heirloom furniture gallery we were standing in. In the *Elle* photo shoot the architecture, and it surely was architecture that provided the setting, white waifs, black waifs, and tan waifs were all sheathed in silver dresses of different cuts, and were caught lounging here and there on the B&B furniture. The person in charge of the shoot understood the house and its light and its potential for display, the subtle skin-like sheen of the walls, the polished black slate floor, and the seductive way light would play off the silver-clad bodies of these unearthly models.

"It's nice outside. Let's go sit by the pool where we can talk," Robert said. I hadn't noticed the pool that stepped down the cliff from where the house sat. "Go on down and I will meet you there." He motioned me to a stairway, a stairway with glass treads and risers that was as ethereal as the house itself. The stair descended through a hole in the floor larger than it needed to be to accommodate the stair, and the stair turned into a piece of sculpture because of the space it was given.

The pool itself was a sheet of coral-colored water with one edge that merged with the horizon. Robert arrived with a tray. He described the contents: Bloody Mary's and bagels and lox. All unfamiliar to me. "Let's eat, and then I'll show you the rest of the house." Robert pulled up a chair beside me. I could tell that this was going to be a lecture. Robert carried on.

"Robert Wilson said . . . do you know who Robert Wilson is?"

"No."

"He's a theater director who studied architecture—no matter. Wilson said, 'Everything begins with light—without light there is no space. And space can't exist without time. They are a part of one thing' . . ."

The rest of his lecture was lost on me as I realized that Robert didn't bring me here to fuck me. He just wanted to mess with my mind. Just being in this house was enough to mess with my mind. How could I put together the two worlds of Robert A. Michael and Reverend Ike, which were galaxies apart?

...

I would spend more and more time working with Reverend Ike on the program for his new facilities. He became a father figure, a father confessor, as it were. I told him about my aspirations to be an architect and how excited I was to be helping his church expand their outreach to the community. But Reverend Ike could be very candid. He said that if I wanted to work in the black community working for Robert might be a handicap. And get real girl. What other community are you going to work for? The fashion industry was the community I really wanted to work for. In my daydreams I was doing boutiques for Versace and Kate Spade. I was busy flying between Milan, New York, London, Paris, and Tokyo, designing on my laptop and the back of bar coasters where all our client/architect meetings would take place. And the bartender would see what we were talking about and see my sketches and tell the owner, who would want me to design her new bar and restaurant. Fashion and food somehow came together in my mind. Inspired by Robert I imagined my architecture to be a set for fashion photo ops. The black community was setting fashion trends. Hip-hop culture had become integrated. This intersection of cultures was where it was at. And so was Reverend Ike's church. The black community had redefined the church just like the black community was redefining fashion. I was black and beautiful and socially conscious and could have been a model and had personality. No reason I couldn't do Reverend Ike's church and a Versace showroom too.

LIQUID ARCHITECTURE

The Cybernaut

Robert was clueless when it came to computer technology. Not intentionally clueless. He could get excited about its prospects. But it was hard to keep his attention. I think he was dyslexic. So probably were Leonardo da Vinci, Louis Kahn, Eero Saarinen, and Richard Rogers. Not bad company to be associated with if you are an architect. I'm dyslexic too. So was Steve Jobs. Ever heard of him? Many architects and brilliant people are.

My role in the office was ambiguous when Robert hired me. I'd like to think I was there to connect Robert A. Michael and Associates, with the future. On a day-to-day basis I managed the office's digital world, which had a way of growing. Robert continually asked me what I was doing on the computer. I had made it clear to him when I wasn't working on studio projects that this was my own stuff. He would get upset if he thought I was using his technology to moonlight for some other office. Of course the temptation was there, but Robert was good to me. He would get me anything I asked for, always afraid that he was slipping behind the expanding field of architectural design and production if he didn't have the latest hardware and software. And when work wasn't pressing, I got to play. I really didn't know how to explain what I was doing to Robert. I gave him some things to read, but I don't know that he ever did. I explained to Robert that I was exploring cyberspace, and his eyes seemed to glaze over. I liked best Marcus Novak's description of cyberspace, and given the ethereal quality of Robert's work I thought Novak's concept of liquidity—liquid architecture—best fit what Robert was trying to do and was something he could understand.

Novak said, "Cyberspace is liquid. Liquid architecture is an architecture that breathes, whose form is contingent on the interests of the beholder; it is an architecture that opens to welcome me and closes to defend me . . . it is an architecture without doors and hallways, where the next room is always where I need it to be and what I need it to be." Robert's architecture, especially his house, which I had seen only twice, once at the annual holiday party and again during my encounter with Medea, seemed to me to be striving to become liquid architecture.

There are so many boundaries in producing architecture. You have a client, who has a program of needs and a building site and preferences for materials and a particular aesthetic, and then there are the externalities, the weather and building codes, etc. And the architect's job is to use his "creativity" to reconcile all these boundaries and produce a building. It's a big fucking deal.

Architects set such restrictions on the way they think. Bucky Fuller opened my eyes to a new way of thinking about the world we live in and our erroneous way of describing it. If the world was flat, he said, we could correctly say "up and down" regarding our relationship to the flat plane we supposedly live on. But we know that the world isn't flat. It is a ball. We live on a sphere with an absolute center surrounded by, as far as we know, infinite space. We should be saying, "Look in" or "Look out." Yet we say look up at the stars. Why? We still struggle using a language inappropriate to the physical facts, as we know them. Would our architecture be different if we said, "Look out at the ceiling"? If we can't deal with the reality of our physical existence in the known universe, how can we deal with an existence in cyberspace, in liquid architecture, where here and there become the same place?

So if we learn from Bucky, we can ask questions like, "What is a door?" A door is to provide access from one space to another. Okay. A door needs a wall. Right? What good is a door without a wall? The earliest modern architects devoted themselves to eliminating the wall and thus the door. Once Robert was looking over my shoulder and said, "Let's get rid of the doors. Let's make the walls open."

"A sliding door?"

"No," he said. "A sliding wall."

That kind of thinking so informed Robert's architecture and that of other modernists like him. But there is still a big jump to be made between this way of thinking and the technologies that can produce liquid architecture. Air curtains are a beginning. A sheet of air can create a permeable barrier between one atmosphere and another while allowing larger objects like people but not smaller objects like insects to pass through. And there are detectors that are used everywhere—libraries, the Gap—where objects are embedded with a code that can set off an alarm if they are passed through a doorless opening. That's what I mean about thinking about the future of architecture. These changes may be ubiquitous, but soon they may affect the way architects think about architecture and the means at their disposal to create the liquid architecture that today ironically is mostly encountered in enclosed shopping malls and airports.

Baudelaire said something like "our common sense tells us that the things of this earth barely exist, that actual reality is only in our dreams." I don't want to deceive you into thinking I actually read Baudelaire, but I read someone who had read him who said that was what he said. I think it's beautiful and profound, so that's why I have remembered it. Actual reality is only in our dreams. Cyberspace is becoming the actual reality of some of our dreams. No up. No down. No in. No out. No time. No place. Just cyberspace.

My favorite way of hitting back at nonbelievers whom I am trying to convert to being cybernauts is to compare cyberspace with heaven and hell. I believe heaven to Catholics and Protestants can be compared to a virtual reality for the good and hell a virtual reality for bad people. Artists have tried to depict heaven, which was a most popular endeavor during the European Renaissance when artists were exploring all kinds of new painterly tricks, early versions of surrealism, as it were. Typical of their fantasies were clouds with angels or cherubs walking or floating in air. St. Peter's pearly gates were depicted as a door without a wall. Liquid architecture turned on itself. Hell, thanks to Dante, was made easier for artists to depict. Besides his apt descriptions borrowed from observing underground grottoes and techniques of torture that were already in practice, he didn't add that much to the narrative of virtual reality, but he inspired visual artists to illustrate his imagination.

My business—I hope it will become my business—is to create these yet-to-be imagined scenarios of cyberspace and to produce virtual realities. I want to add sound to my mix. At one end of the sound spectrum is silence, the kind of silence broken by the sounds of a butterfly's wings, so soft one can imagine that it is a sound made by an angel. At the other end is the sound produced by a rock band with the bass amp turned way up. The bass is so strong that you can feel it pounding against your chest, and the sound feels like it has taken control of your body and makes your bones dance. In between somewhere are sounds created by a train conductor applying the brakes to a subway train, metal on metal, not dissimilar to the sound of fingernails across the chalkboard remembered from childhood that split your head open. Your head. Not your ears. Your head. Or more pleasantly for me the sound of high heels on a hard surface. Click, click . . . click, click. You can feel the hips moving and the breasts doing their bump da bump thing, all virtually of course. How many cinematic versions of this can you recall? Movie directors proceed from one scene to another with just a few seconds of the sound that accompanies that next scene, clueing you into what to expect. Listen carefully the next time you go to the movies. Sound is very important in the making of virtual reality. Hollywood has known that for a long time, ever since the "talkie," which wasn't just about talking. Virtual sounds can give us virtual spatial clues.

Have you heard of James Turrell? He is God. He has taken heaven and brought it right down here to earth. That's a metaphor. Not in pictures, not in words, not in objects but in what for some seems like reality. Ancient civilizations have known of the tricks Turrell uses. There are historic places in India, in Ireland, in Egypt, and there are the structures in Chaco Canyon in New Mexico created by a civilization now lost. Imagine the world without light pollution. I have only lived in places with light pollution, but I visited Chaco Canyon. You are not allowed entry at night. But we did get in. Lying there at night looking through the openings created long ago by the Anasazi Indians the sky becomes an animated picture. The colors within the opening change so intensely. That is what Turrell is able to create. He understands color. He will cut out a piece of a ceiling, and you sit there looking out and watch the sky change from white to blue, to orange, to black, and these transitional colors in between. There is no doubt you are looking "out," thanks to Turrell's magical creation. By erasing part of the observed universe, what remains becomes more vivid. Of course this isn't new. The oculus in the Roman Pantheon! Wow! Can you imagine being "in" one of these colors? You are covered in the color, and the color has dimension to it. Turrell's work verifies that.

I say all this because I don't think we are that far from creating cyberspace. The bits and pieces and thinking have already arrived. Our biggest obstacle is lack of imagination. There are some concepts you have to put behind you. Get away from your anthropomorphized thinking. So here is my world. Why not develop a vision similar to what flies have where you can experience lots of images all at once or vision that allows you to see history? When you look at something you can see its history. Why not incorporate time into how we see? We have machines with x-ray vision and electromagnetic imaging, so why not, in our cyberspace world, give everyone that ability? We can gather so much more information by incorporating these three simple concepts into our world. I am sure that there are people presently working on these very ideas.

I don't imagine cyberspace being anything like the space we know. Being a cybernaut is like getting into a plane without knowing how to fly and figuring it out as you go along. Robert thought I was unique, but there is a world of people like me out there. It is a multicultural, multiethnic, multispatial, multigenerational (though mostly young), multigendered (though mostly male) world of people doing the same thing I am doing. We are creating our own cyber society because we believe we can do this. We know we can do this. My generation will be the one to realize the full possibility of liquid architecture.

Robert sometimes would kick around other architects' offices just to see what was going on. One day he returned with an idea for the space I would occupy. He thought of it as a kind of promotion that I would get my own space. The space was to be a three-dimensional grid. He described it as a 3D net. When it was built it looked more like the pen some people keep their dogs in. He asked me what I thought. I dunno. What was I supposed to think? He liked it. He was the boss, at least of the real space of the office. Was he afraid I was going to infect the office and this was an opportunity to pen me up? When the dog gets led to the pen does it care as long as it is fed? I lived in the computer not with the computer. Why would I care what kind of real space I occupied?

The grid became my home. Other people had computers, but I was the boss when it came to computers. And I had the boss's office now, inside the grid. Anyone who wanted to see me had to come inside the grid. Got a problem with your computer? Come inside the grid. The grid pixilated the space inside, and I think that is what Robert liked about it. It simulated the world before high-definition TV or high-resolution computers or smart phones or other mobile devices. It gave the appearance one has of looking at a Chuck Close portrait up close, composed of his carefully constructed matrix of complex painted dots. It messed with time and space. Was it Robert's way of saying he didn't quite see the cyber world the way I did? I began to change my world to become a little more invisible in my black grid. Here I was in this pixilated space in my black jeans and tees, black socks and Doc Martens, being nearly invisible, I thought.

But apparently I wasn't invisible to Medea. When Robert brought her from New York, she was given her own desk and phone in the studio, and we were told that she was doing marketing, like we were manufacturing stuff that people needed to know about so they could buy it? She was into producing brochures, etc. Mostly the old way, cut and paste and print to make each one appear to be custom made for whoever the next John might be. I told her I could help these look more finished and professional by scanning them into the computer and saving her time. Not too much later she was doing content and I was in charge of design and production as she trolled for clients and publicity. Photoshop can produce its own cyberspace.

One memorable afternoon, she approached the grid and said, "Naut"—that was what everyone called me—"Naut, I would like to talk with you. Can we have lunch?" Can we have lunch! It was after the noon hour but before the usual office lunch break. Everyone in the office took a break around one o'clock. She knew that I always brought my own lunch, so her question must mean eating out.

We got into her BMW. She wanted to go across town for some reason. I later found out why. She had brought along a picnic lunch, she said, and we went to a park near the topmost part of Abercrombie Heights, past all these fucking McMansions that turned my stomach. Her BMW said she belonged here among the doctors and lawyers, techno tycoons, media people, and achievers who occupied the pretend villas. She stopped at a roadside outcrop that had room for just one car. She pulled a hamper from the back of the car and spread a cloth below a tree. From the hamper she pulled out a bottle of wine, glasses, and sandwiches. What was this? This looked like something she and Robert might do.

She obviously had this spot all picked out. This was no accident. She propped herself against a giant maple tree with her legs apart and her knees poking above her skirt, her milky white legs like a dancer's. And she asked me if I had any meetings that afternoon. Meetings? She knew I never had a "meeting" with anyone except herself and sometimes Robert to talk about projects. He was out of town. She could see the quizzical look on my face. "Then relax," she said. "There's no hurry to get back to the studio."

She opened the bottle of wine and passed me the sandwiches. She poured both of us wine in these very nice goblets and said, "Here is a toast to cyberspace." I thought here is a toast to the space between your legs. I hadn't touched the wine, but I felt dizzy just being this close to her away from the studio. I felt like a virgin and totally out of my element. I was disarmed and sitting in this spot sitting on the edge of the horizon, just the two of us, at her mercy.

I can't remember what we talked about. She kept asking me about cyberspace and virtual reality. She told me she thought it was the most important thing to happen to communication since the invention of the printing press. She insisted on pouring me more wine. She kept on and on with the questions and spoke softer and softer. She asked if I smoked and then rolled a joint. We picked up the stuff and got back to the car, and she said she had to stop by Robert's house for a minute to pick up something. I had only seen the house during the holiday party, and it was so filled with people and sounds from a DJ that it was hard to really experience the architecture. She asked me to come in . . . it wouldn't take long, and we drove through the gate and there was this shimmering transparency of glass you could see through to eternity. The horizon and the sky melted into each other. She led me down some stairs and out to a pool, which was oh so wet and cool looking and said for me to wait. Descending the stairs had made me dizzy. She was back in a minute, and when I heard her footsteps, which now sounded like sandaled feet, I turned around to see her standing there naked. Gloriously naked, the kind of vision that one gets of a woman just around puberty. Was this a wine-and-drug-induced dream? *Fuck, man, what is happening here*? She walked over to me and unbuttoned my shirt and then kneeled down and took off my shoes and unzipped my fly and took out my cock and started sucking it, and jeez . . . dream or nightmare, I didn't want it to stop . . . *what if Robert finds out? . . . there goes my job . . . my . . . but, oh my God . . . I would just as soon die right here . . . if this were my very last moment on earth it would be okay* . . . and I was about to come and she moved me around and pushed me into the pool, which was warm and then she was on top of me and she was riding me and I was coming and drowning and I didn't know which was going to happen first, but I came and gasped. She grabbed my head and stuck it in her crotch and let out a moan, which I thought was made by an animal standing on the edge of the pool and watching us, and then we were floating, kind of cradling each other, and her skin was so smooth and soft, both supple and firm and strong, and her hair all matted and her smile . . . and she had this smile that said . . . I had a good time, hope you didn't mind. She left the pool like an accomplished swimmer does, as though some unseen hand was just lifting her up. She was standing over me with water dripping from her nipples and pubic hair, and she swung her head so her hair flung water in every direction. "Just a minute and

I will get you a towel." She returned in a black silk robe that clung to her, accentuating the shape of her body, a black-on-black canvas similar to the Ad Reinhardt painting I would be shown later. And then she said it: "I hope you didn't mind?" Jeezez Christ, she didn't even ask me if I could swim. She produced a thermos of coffee.

She was so cool. It was like we had just been introduced even though we had been working together for a while, and there we were sitting naked—me anyway, except for the towel—and she was asking me questions about virtual reality all over again. "Was fucking in the pool anything like virtual sex?" she wanted to know. I said I didn't know; I had just read about virtual sex and didn't know if anyone had actually experienced it yet, though movies like *Lawnmower Ma*n and *Brainstorm* had tried to stimulate it . . . Did I say stimulate? I meant simulate. It was more a concept though some of the tools were available, like the data glove. I explained that she could be here and I could be . . . well, even back in my grid, and I would put on this glove with lots of data points and she would be wearing a body suit with sensors that could feel the movement of my hand. I could see her getting excited . . . again. I knew that people were working on creating gloves and suits and other hardware that were both sensors and effectors, ah, input-output devices to use ancient computer lingo. Once perfected, the dildo would never be the same.

We got back in the pool. It was starting to get dark when she lit up another joint. She asked me to stay over. Jeezez, if Robert ever found out. "He won't," she said. She drove me up there. It would take me half a night to walk home, even if I could find my way. If I was her new media guru and sex slave, so be it. As the writer R. U. Sirius wrote, "We have kicked the Reality Syndrome once and for all." At least I had for the moment.

Medea knew more about digital technology than she let on. She confessed that she was fascinated with sensual pleasure for as long as she could remember . . . ever since she first touched herself. She had been a Timothy Leary groupie for a while. She had done all kinds of drugs, most I had never heard of, chemical stuff, but now she just smoked pot. She loved architecture because it could bring you a high, something she hadn't known until she experienced Robert's house. She described the reflections, the changes of color with the rising moving and setting sun, the shift to moonlight, the starlight, light through a mist, lightning and its stereoscopic quality, reflected light off white walls as well as black tile, and the swarmy light bouncing off the water in the pool onto the ceiling over the bed. Did Robert and Medea have this conversation after the first time he made love to her there? If he had, she was a good pupil. As the city's lights faded, the reflected light from the pool danced on the ceiling above the bed just as she said it would. Medea was on top, so I could watch.

THE BUSINESS OF BUSINESS

The Son

Dad was livid when I told him I wanted to get my MBA and go into real estate and possibly development. "Goddamn it. Chip," he said. "You don't need a goddamned MBA to sell real estate. You don't even need any brains to sell real estate. Real estate sales has become the field for bored housewives and out-of-work Tupperware salesmen." His words were stinging.

"But, Dad," I replied, "Grandfather sold real estate, and he told me he wanted you to go into real estate."

"And your grandfather didn't have an MBA. He had to drop out of college because of the Depression, and he was lucky to be in the right place at the right time and happened on some land to sell and someone to buy it and he thought he had his ticket to heaven. Your grandfather could have sold anything to anyone. He had all those qualities you and I don't have, the gift of gab, the ability to tell a story, and the ability to exaggerate the truth when necessary. Nobody is going to buy real estate from you because you have an MBA."

I thought hard about Dad's remarks. Grandfather did have those qualities that Dad and I lacked. He was always full of jokes, for one. He seemed to have several for each occasion. An incredible storehouse of them was kept in his brain filed and ready to project on his retinas as though they were computer screens with unlimited access to a huge store of well-catalogued jokes and puns. Grandfather also had a fertile imagination. He was creative in a unique way—a matchmaker in one sense, matching up people with property. If the match wasn't just right, he would make it right by ascribing attributes to the property or the potential buyer that might be lacking, creating a narrative that would seal the deal. And Grandfather's customers were always satisfied, being sold on seeing things in a property no one else could see, or imagining themselves taking on the attributes Grandfather thought suited them as would-be owners of such and such a property.

Dad and I both had good imaginations, but when it came to expressing ourselves verbally we were at a loss. Dad could turn ideas into buildings. What he had difficulty putting into words he could draw. He couldn't draw up emotions, of course. Those most often were kept locked up, at least the ones that were most important. I was the same way. But he could draw. He loved to draw. He said he kept a journal, but his journal was really a sketchbook that he carried with him all the time. This wordless journal was full of sketches filled with his ideas and observations. His sketches might include just doodles made of fantastic shapes and lines. He could sketch the face of a child he'd seen days earlier and was able to recall and in a moment of reflection fill a page of his sketchbook with this memory. His sketchbook was his way of capturing the world. Like a net others might use to catch butterflies, Dad's sketchbook captured anything that he would consider worth recording. He much admired the notebooks of the great masters, Leonardo, Michelangelo, and others. Our library was full of books of their work, and when he was pensive or in one of his periods of depression, he would get these books out and pick a sketch and try to copy its every detail. I found him doing this one-day, and he confided that this was his way of escaping the world. He said, "Chip, when I look at a Leonardo drawing and I take out my pen and paper and I imagine what Leonardo was seeing or thinking when he was drawing, I can become Leonardo for a moment." He would fall silent and then go back to drawing. That was all the explanation I needed he felt. Drawing was a drug for Dad, and he would return to his reverie as though someone had plunged a hypodermic needle into his arm. "Why didn't I become an artist?" he once asked me in one of his dream states.

I knew that Dad loved his father, but he had no love for his father's occupation. I was just a kid when Grandfather sold one of Dad's first houses on spec, but we heard the story all the time. Like an author Grandfather invented people for the houses Dad designed and then went out searching for their flesh and blood.

Dad told me that he never had to think of people inhabiting the houses he designed. Early in his professional life when he was doing spec houses for Grandfather he accepted that that was his father's role. Instead he was free to think about proportions, materials, lightness and light, and the horizon. The rooms in which certain activities might take place were incidental to the larger concept of the house. "People will discover how to use it" was one of Dad's favorite sayings. But for the unimaginative client, Grandfather's narrative and vast supply of jokes would fill the gap between the object Dad created and the utilitarian vessel that the unsuspecting homeowner was looking for. Invariably, the homeowners did, as Dad imagined, discover how to use their houses. Many owners became lifelong friends and future clients as their families grew and they wanted a larger house or addition. But Dad never forgave them deep down inside, in his own self-defeating way, for having been conned by his father, who received more in compensation for the real estate transaction than Dad received for design of their residence.

I tried to explain to Dad that the real estate business had changed. It wasn't simply based on whom you knew and how charming you could be, but it had become a science, especially for someone like me who was interested in commercial real estate. You needed to know something about finance, you needed to know something about planning, you needed to know something about land use law and codes, you had to know something about business trends, and you even needed to know something about architecture. An MBA was invaluable to understanding this sophisticated world. Besides, I would be working with others with MBAs. I would need to know their language and have a degree they respected.

Dad didn't put up much of a fight. When I was in my early teens, he had confessed to me, in what I thought was going to be one of those father-son talks that never happened, that he had hoped the brother I had never met, Robert Jr., would have become an architect and his partner. That dream died with Robert Jr.—a nontransferable dream. Perhaps he shared this story with me because it was clear I had none of my brother's attributes. I didn't like to draw, not even the crayon doodles that every kid is forced to create for the refrigerator door to demonstrate the child's latent creative genius. No, I didn't do that. And I showed no interest in what Dad did, even though he would take my sister and me to his office some Sunday mornings to get us out of the house. My sister would sit at one of the empty drafting tables and draw as she was supposed to. I read. Dad knew there was no hope of my becoming an architect and no sense in forcing the issue.

That I wanted to go into the real estate business, however, wasn't just distasteful; I wanted to be the antichrist in his mind. And he wasn't even religious. I knew that I had no hope of changing my father's mind about the career I wanted. If I was successful in my chosen field, he would hate me for being in a field he despised. If I failed, he would tell me that he told me so.

Dad had his ironic side. One of his favorite habits was to give us books with hidden or not-so-hidden meanings, often revealed by an inscription he would write on the title page. A gift he gave me on my birthday before I departed for graduate school was Donald Trump's *The Art of the Deal.* Inside Dad had inscribed "To Chip: Please don't bring embarrassment to the family name or your profession as this man has to his. Love Dad." The inscription was written in block letters, and under them, where it said "Love Dad," were his initials, RAM, and the date.

I understood the business side of architecture somewhat from watching Dad's struggles with his studio. He would never call his work a business or the place he worked an office. Perhaps that was one reason his enterprise was so erratic. In my lifetime there were several recessions. The first was when Dad was still designing spec houses for Grandfather. He had to operate out of his home. I was just a little squirt, but I remember him being home a lot. He opened the office in Printer's Row as things got better and he got commissions on his own. A second recession was the bust in the eighties when his office of twelve became six and even his church work dried up. He confided, and maybe this is worth knowing, "For me the glass was always half-full. I would have my people just doing stuff with no accounts receivable, and then I would wake up to realize there was a lot of outgo but no income. I would rant and rave at Ms. Jones, and she would remind me that she had asked for a meeting months before to discuss 'the problem' and I would say no, things would get better. Then she told me that the last payroll checks would bounce if I didn't put some money in the business account. Then she got her meeting. And then I had to let people go. It broke my heart." I believe that he told me this as a way of saying he hadn't provided for his family as he would have liked and his office staff were part of his family. I think secretly that he hoped I would do better.

He and Mom separated during one of these recessions when he borrowed money from her parents and told her he didn't intend to pay them back. He thought they should "invest" him.

Al Darling was a classmate of mine whose father was already in the real estate business. Residential. His father had read about "new urbanism" and knew that my father was an architect. On a visit to campus one weekend he asked me about my dad and what kind of architecture he did. Al's dad had 180 acres of property outside of Chicago that had been in the family for years. He thought the time was ripe to develop it, but he wanted to do something different than the usual five—or ten-acre single-family development. He had read a publication that suggested that "new urbanism" was a way a developer might make money in a tight real estate market. The family had already done some traditional subdivision work on the orchard property they owned. "Been there done that," Al's dad told me. He was ready for something more venturesome.

I mentioned meeting Al's father to my dad on one of my breaks and told Dad that he was interested in new urbanism, asking if he knew anything about it. His face just turned into a scowl. *End of that*, I thought. It was at our graduation that our fathers met. I saw them talking after Al had introduced them to each other, and then they disappeared. Back at the hotel, I saw them in the bar in animated conversation. They seemed to be getting along. Dad said he remembered my mentioning this guy and he seemed not to be such a bad chap so he had asked him about his plans for a new urbanist community, and he told Dad that he was still looking for an architect. Dad couldn't resist the temptation to learn more, especially when his senses were telling him that the economy was going to take a turn for the worse and a project of this scope could keep his studio in business for several years. They arranged to meet at the site thirty miles northwest of Chicago over the next weekend.

Dad said, "This is about building a community, son. I am reminded of Frank Lloyd Wright's ideas for Broad Acre City and Ludwig Hilberseimer's sketches for rational communities. It was part of the modern movement's tradition to think big, to think at the scale of communities, and this just might be my chance to put it all together, to do what I've always wanted to do, to build a community of my very own design." Dad had never mentioned wanting to design a community before, but now he had embraced this opportunity, an opportunity that seemed to be within his grasp.

I had work to finish at school. Even though I had "graduated," I still had an incomplete paper, so it was a couple of weeks later when I saw Dad again. "How'd it go?" I asked.

Mockingly, Dad said, "How did what go?" knowing exactly that I was referring to his meeting with Mr. Darling. When Dad started acting like this, I knew he was excited about something and just wanted to drag out the conversation.

The meeting was "fantastic," he said. The property was beautiful, with a stream, some woods, and a rolling terrain that had once been an orchard. It was perfect. No expressway noises to berm, no power lines to try to ignore, no brownfields, no environmental stuff to speak of. The land had been in the Darling family for a very long time. They had held it anticipating that the city would come to them. It had. Now it was time to build, and Mitch (Mitch Darling, Al's father) was ready to do something that his long-deceased great-grandfather, who had acquired the land, would be proud of. They discussed how a new urbanism development might fit the land, and Dad agreed to make some sketches of his ideas for the place before they talked about a contract. He was so excited that he couldn't wait to get the property survey and the aerial photographs. They had discussed doing the project in phases. That suited Dad just fine. He could see this project taking maybe five or six years, enough time to see him through the recession economists were forecasting. He wanted to "get this guy Darling wrapped up as a client," he said. I thought to myself, *Then get a contract, Dad. Don't start giving away your services right off the bat.* But I held my tongue.

As a friend of Al's, I heard both sides of this story. Al and I had stayed in touch. You know how it is the first year after graduation. You have this love-hate relationship with those who had been your buddies. You wish them well, as long as they don't get a better job than you. I was golden. A brokerage firm hired me to manage a real estate investment trust. I couldn't believe it. They paid off my graduate school debt, paid for my relocation costs, and gave me a $50,000 signing bonus. That was as good as lawyers were getting.

Al decided to accept his father's invitation to work for him. In fact, the project he was going to be managing was the "new urbanism" community Dad was working on, though Dad never used the words "new urbanism."

It took awhile for the project to be given a name. They were stuck with Darling because they wanted to honor Mitch's great-grandfather and of course the family name. But Darling "whatever" could end up sounding pretty coy. After considering many alternatives: Darling Acres, Darling Meadows, Darling Lakes (they would have to create them), they settled on Dad's suggestion, Darling Mews. It was named after the street and alley system he had already designed that gave the development a character very different from any suburban development—a land-development pattern favored by new urbanists and a reflection of a centuries-old English system of urban development that placed stables, later converted to garages, at the rear of dwellings below carriage houses. The twentieth century saw these traditional developments turned into some of the most coveted high-end properties in London. Mitch and Al bought into the name with little convincing. They liked the association.

Dad finally had the opportunity to build what he saw as a prototype of the new American suburb, which would offer individual privacy and private ownership in a dense development that would preserve a picturesque country setting. Based on his interpretation of the mews idea, houses had front courtyards and rear alleys. Instead of the typical "in your face" garages of the suburbs, garages were tucked in the back, making the fronts of the houses friendlier—more walkable.

With Dad's concept approved, the Darlings drew up a contract to work with my father. Then the trouble began. The contract stipulated that Dad's firm wouldn't be paid until the first units were sold. The Darlings were asking Dad to participate in the risk. But Dad had people to pay, he had drawings to do, and he would have 90 percent of his work completed before the first unit sold. He couldn't wait that long. His hope for this recession-proof contract was fading. "Okay," the Darlings said. "We will give you a piece of the action." In return for his services, the Darlings proposed giving Dad a percentage of the ownership of the project that he could later sell when the project was completed. Before that, he could use his partial ownership to get a bank loan so he could pay his staff and his other expenses. The Darlings said they would even set him up with their bank contact, and they did.

Dad didn't anticipate the time it would take to get the zoning approvals from the township. Of course he had been through this before with all the single family houses he had designed and seen through construction. There was always this or that to deal with during the project review, and he always made sure to work within the codes unless it was impossible, which it was on some difficult sites like Amy and Andy's house.

But this was country. Raw country. Country country. Not-In-My-Back Yard, NIMBY country. Territory who's elected officials saw themselves as caretakers of where the buffalo and Indians had once roamed. This was a township that had only just recently passed a zoning amendment that would allow planned-unit developments, PUDs, and the kind of zoning that the Darlings would need to develop Darling Mews. This would be the township's first such development. It would test the law, and it would outrage all those good citizens who were opposed to the law in the first place. Why couldn't this property be developed like all the rest of the township, houses on five—and ten-acre lots, minimum? The enlightened citizens of the township saw the future come barreling down on them. Developments proposing one-acre lots, not ten acres, were becoming more common as land became scarce and more expensive, the houses bigger, the lots smaller, and the city closer. Soon they thought they would have McMansions built on one-acre lots. Township officials would have preferred keeping the zoning as it had always been (they claimed), but a lawsuit was brought by the local chapter of the ACLU that argued that existing zoning was discriminating against the building of housing for people with more modest incomes. The township didn't stand a chance. So the PUD was a way for the township-planning commission to get back control of development. They knew that most of the choice sites that were left had been acquired by developers who would love the opportunity to use the PUD zoning as a way of getting more development on the land. But developers would have to get planning approval on all development using PUD zoning, which would be voted up or down by the planning commission. The planning commission was back in control of the township, and they relished the opportunity to delay projects and force changes against the developer's wishes. Dad was no longer in control of the future of Darling Mews.

The Darlings ceded the responsibility for obtaining planning commission approval to Robert A. Michael, and Associates, Architects. Dad resented this responsibility, which required him to make appearances at planning commission meetings an hour-and-a-half drive away that often lasted late into the weekday evening. Dad had to do battle over where retaining ponds would be located, where access roads from the main arterial could be located, and how streets were to be configured to allow fire and emergency vehicles access, and after each planning commission meeting there were new questions and challenges. "Those politically appointed know-nothing idiots on the planning commission have never read a book on planning, know nothing about what is current in planning literature, and are there simply out of meanness with their desire to stop any development in the township. Fuck them!" Those were Dad's words verbatim. He was becoming a stronger supporter of new urbanism planning principles than he would ever have imagined, a fact he would never admit to except in conversation with the Darlings.

APPROPRIATING VALUE

The Developer

I like Robert. I really do. I mean I like him like you'd like a stray dog or a stray cat. No, a stray dog. Strays stay faithful if you treat them right, though you'd never treat them like one of your own. Robert wasn't one of us, you know. We could never be buddy-buddy, though we had some things in common it seems. He told me that his father was a realtor. That's not the same as being a developer, but I guess his father did some development in his day. Robert said he never liked developers because of that, until he met us.

We—Al, my son, and I and my father and his father before him—are people of the land. Landed gentry, some might say. When Great-grandfather came over, that was almost all he had—just some land that was given to him by the government. Yes, it was a fact that he had been educated at Oxford and that made him a gentleman. That education elevated him to the diplomatic corps and led him to the colonies. He fell in love with the land of the new world and wanted to stay and headed west to find his own. The Darlings have always been gentlemen. Al's children will be descended from gentlemen. Darling means gentlemen to many people. Grandfather was a husband to the land in the great English tradition. That was an approach the native Indians had toward the land as well. They were caretakers of the land. They were dependent upon the land just as we are. Grandfather cherished every acre and tended to its proper maintenance and care. He loved trees. He might have been a cousin to Johnny Appleseed. Orchards were his passion. He didn't have much of a love for crops or cattle. To him an orchard was a way of using the land's potential for productivity and creating a landscape different from God's, and better, in his mind. "A thing of beauty the orchard," he often said. An orchard with its evenly spaced trees planted in neat roles was a way of bringing order to an unruly landscape.

The time came when the next generation had the chance to escape from the land and the time-consuming labor it took to be a husband to the land. My father told me that he moved to the city to seek his fortune only to be called back to the land by the Depression. The family sold land, gave it away really, as a way to stay alive then. The orchards declined because there wasn't money to take care of them. But we are all an educated family. Each generation has gone to college. Maybe not Oxford by any means, but Al, my son, has an MBA from the best business school in America, and America has the best. This here is where business was invented. Or should I say reinvented because of the opportunities the land provided.

Robert didn't seem to be interested in golf or riding or hunting. Those were sports that were a part of our family heritage. Robert was more interested in team sports—this team and that team, which were mostly horse manure to me. I think Robert really envied us our sports that nurtured individual accomplishments. You, playing golf against your own personal best score. When you played with others, you played with a handicap, a concept Robert didn't seem to understand. You and the horse, you and the gun and the bird. Thank God none of us Darlings was forced into participating in any of those team sports. Al almost was. He stands six four, so everyone thought he was a natural for basketball. But as he says, in a not-too-delicate way, for him, trying to dribble a basketball was like trying to dribble a ball of horse manure. We had others who would shovel and dribble our horse manure.

Robert had a funny way of looking at the world. He was the first architect I had worked with. He convinced me that he could make a contribution to our project. But when it came to his compensation, we started miles apart. He proposed a flat fee for the planning part based on his estimate of the hours it would take him to create a plan and for the architectural part a fee based on the percentage of the cost of each housing unit. I really thought he was screwing himself, but I said okay. Then he wanted 25 percent of the estimated planning costs up front, as a retainer. I knew that we were going to have a problem then. I was going to build this project not with my money but the bank's. If I was going to risk my hide and the bank was going to risk theirs, then Robert could sure as hell risk his too. He didn't see it that way. He was a professional, he said. Hell, I said, even lawyers provide their services at risk, and they clean up. Look at all the successful ambulance chasers out there.

I couldn't follow Robert's reasoning. The project was going to be worth more in total than the cost of each house, but he was basing his fee on the construction cost rather than the sale cost. And the most money was to be made on the land's development; taking an orchard and turning it into a subdivision with streets, utilities, and all that gave it a value ten times what it started as, and he was just going to charge us an hourly fee for turning that land into something ten times as valuable. It didn't figure, but I didn't try to explain that he was undervaluing what his contribution could be worth.

The cold hard fact was we didn't have any money to pay him. Not that we are poor folk. No, we've got money in the bank and enough to pay Robert a hundred times over for this project. But in this world every tub is on its own bottom. Each project is its own incorporated entity, so if there is a failure, God forbid, it doesn't harm other ventures. So each project starts with the land, and the idea is to add value to the land and when you sell it all off you take the difference between what the land was valued at and what your construction costs were along with all the soft costs like insurance and interest and fees and permits and such and the difference is your profit or God forbid your loss.

Finances weren't the half of it with Robert. There was his damn architecture to deal with, and that is what got the project in trouble. If his son and mine weren't such good friends . . . well, damn it, frankly Robert wouldn't have lasted a week past his preliminary sketches. Don't get me wrong. We liked his site plan. It used the new urbanism principles we wanted him to consider. Even the civil engineer liked it. Took fewer roads and less utilities; took less grading, took fewer trees, and it was efficient. Just what we wanted, and it put more units on the site than we imagined originally.

But let me tell you about his architecture. To begin with we were looking for something, you know, historic. The Darling name and all that being so tied to English history we were looking for something like an English country village. I'd seen this picture of a project in England, Poundberry or something like that in Wales, designed by this new urbanist architect for the Prince of Wales. That was just what we wanted, though we couldn't have used the fancy brickwork and details they used in Poundberry. Too expensive. But that was the spirit of the place we wanted. That was what we had in the back of our minds. Saw it in *Architectural Digest*. We saw Darling Mews taking its place in that same magazine in a couple of years.

Well, let me tell you what Robert showed us in his sketches for Darling Mews. First there were all these damn flat roofs. Not a single pitched roof in the whole lot. They looked more like apartment buildings than houses. "Who is going to pay us a half million dollars for something that looks like an apartment building, and not a pretty apartment building at that?" I questioned him.

I remember the meeting we had at the country club. We planned it as a cordial evening. Cocktails were scheduled for 6:30, and these were to be followed by a presentation by Robert followed by dinner with our wives around eight o'clock. The bank was there, and our accountants and lawyer were there, all with their wives of course, and we had invited some friends who had shown an interest in what we were proposing and were prospective buyers or investors of course.

I introduced the project and talked about the land and how important it was to Grandfather and our family's heritage and all that and our vision for the property and I talked a little about Poundberry and our own vision or whatever, which we had seen in *Architectural Digest*, and then I turned it over to Robert.

Robert got up, and he didn't have any drawings with him. No easels, no nothing, just a computer sitting on a desk next to a projector and a guy I hadn't met before. Robert pulled a screen down from the ceiling.

Robert wasn't a master with words. Oh, he could be eloquent, but he always appeared a little nervous and clumsy in front of people. But this evening he seemed confident. He stood in front of the screen and said nice things about the Darling family, how happy he was to be given this opportunity, how he'd put his very heart and soul into this project, how it was the opportunity of a lifetime, etc., etc. Then he introduced this kid who had been sitting beside the computer. He had black jeans and a black T-shirt on, with diamond stud earrings and a tattoo on his neck and God knows what else you couldn't see that might have been tattooed or pierced. It only made you wonder. Then Robert introduced him as "our cybernaut." *What's a cybernaut?* I thought. The cybernaut was going to fly us through the virtual Darling Mews. We were about to experience virtual reality. *Oh fuck,* I thought, *I hope this doesn't make us sick.*

Robert turned the lights down. The room was dark, and I became aware of the hum of the computer. A tiny spot appeared on the screen and slowly got bigger and music began. I recognized it from that *2001: A Space Odyssey* thing by a famous classical composer. The Chicago Symphony had played it once. The image got bigger, and soon it was big enough so you could see that it was the earth, and as the earth rotated the image zoomed in on England and then across to North America and pulled up over Chicago and began to zoom in and became an aerial view of the site and the music was building and just as the music went *ta-da,* these buildings seemed to pop out of the ground. It was Darling Mews.

Suddenly the image tipped, and I could feel those who'd had too much to drink feeling nauseous. As the image tipped, the music changed into this whishing sound and we seemed to be flying down the street between the houses. But the houses all looked like apartment buildings. They had flat roofs. I had told Robert no flat roofs. But there they were, flat roofs. And where were the windows? The exterior walls were all transparent, and you could see right inside. And, as I thought that, we flew inside through the glass wall and past the entrance hall and the living room, through the dining room, the kitchen, the great space, the den, and the master bedroom and into the master bath, and there in the Jacuzzi there was this luscious broad taking a bath. The women in the audience gasped and started whispering to each other. The woman in the bath got out of the tub, and now it was obvious that she was a computerized version, because she was walking in kind of a herky-jerky way, but she had all her parts. *What an ass,* I thought to myself. And we followed her out onto the balcony and saw what she saw: flat roofs with potted plants on them.

Then in a death-defying ascent, we got tilted up and took off and did a few more flybys, strafing Darling Mews as though it were some military base. It looked like a military base. A blast of music and now we saw the heaven and there was a full moon that we were heading for, and there was a face in the full moon, and as we got closer, I saw that the face was mine. Who the hell did Robert think he was, putting my face on the moon? The face in the moon was smiling. Mine was not as Robert turned the lights up.

The people in our small little audience were turning and looking at each other. Robert stood there as though he was expecting applause or some kind of acknowledgment and didn't say anything. The cybernaut stood and turned. Expecting something? Instead people were whispering to each other. I couldn't hear what they were saying. I was too distracted. I stood and looked toward Robert. "Is that all?" I asked, hoping it was and wasn't.

"That is all for now," Robert said. "Unless there are any questions." People went right on talking to each other, and then slowly silence fell across the room. It became so silent that you could hear people's heads turn as they stared at Robert and his cybernaut as though they were alien creatures that had arrived from another planet. The silence was unbearable. I thought each second was costing me thousands of dollars as I felt the loyalty to the project that had once filled the room slipping away across the eighteenth hole. "Robert," I think I said, "perhaps questions can wait until dinner." The party exited the room quietly. Robert seemed perplexed. I wanted to throttle him on the spot, right there and then.

As the last guest left, I closed the door behind them. "What the hell was that all about?" I said.

"It was a surprise. I thought you would like it," Robert responded.

"Surprise, my ass. It was a nightmare. You just put us through a nightmare. It may be your dream, but it is our nightmare. I thought we were clear about what this project was going to look like. I showed you pictures of that place called Poundberry. Poundberry will sell around here. It honors my father and my grandfather and our whole frigging origins. And if you don't do it, then I'll get the frigging Prince of Wales and his frigging architect, that Krier guy, over here to do it for us. Do you understand?"

There were times when Robert could make you believe he was descended from heaven to do God's work here on earth. That he was God's own architect. He had that look of astonishment on his face. How could I be questioning what he had just showed us? How could I suggest that I might hire someone else? How could I suggest that the project be something other than what he imagined it being?

"Look," I said, "I'm too upset to discuss it now. Our guests are waiting. When you get in there, you tell them that you and Mr. Darling are still discussing the project. You can say I love your site plan, but the architecture, the architecture still needs some work. Got it? And, as for your spiked and tattooed cybernaut, I don't want him at the table. Here's a ten. Tell him to go get a burger somewhere his costume will be appreciated." Robert was visibly upset. I was pleased that my words had some effect on him. "And I'll see you at my office at 7:00 tomorrow. I'll have some rolls and coffee ready. That's 7:00 a.m.!"

The dinner was an uncomfortable affair. Robert sat at one end of our table and I at the other. No one talked to Robert or me. Instead my wife astutely took over the conversation, as she knew how, talking about the symphony, the museum fund drive, and our planned trip to Wales to see architecture.

Robert arrived the next day at a quarter to eight carrying his Starbucks coffee in one hand and a cardboard tube that held rolled-up drawings in the other. My staff had eaten all the rolls, and what was left of the coffee was cold. Our coffee wasn't good enough for Robert anyway. So what was so frigging special about Starbucks coffee? Overpriced, overhyped. I preferred tea. Darjeeling tea. Almost rhymed with Darling.

Robert already knew how I felt. I was going to let him do the talking. How did I feel? I felt betrayed. It was just one of those things. How can I explain? You expect one thing and you get another. My wife did that to me all the time, and I resented it. At every big event she'd ask me what she should wear. I'd tell her what I thought. Then she'd model a dress that fit my description, and I would say I adored it, and then she'd wear something else. It was as though she was testing me to see what I liked so she could do the opposite. And the something else was always provocative, showing too much shoulder, too much back, too much cleavage. Where did she get those dresses anyway? She never modeled those, but they would appear. A minute before we were to leave for whatever, there she was on the stairs, beautiful and showing too much skin. What her body looked like was between her and me. She didn't have to show it off to anyone. I wasn't a prude. But she was my wife and she didn't have to be on the make to our friends. What was she trying to prove? She was no longer young, but she was still beautiful. She didn't have to show so much skin to prove it.

Robert was playing the same bait-and-switch game with me. He'd shown me something that I thought looked like Poundberry just days before. Then this, this military base complete with a battle simulation that turned everyone's stomach. And my face in the moon, and that cyber woman in the bath who, come to think of it, looked a lot like my wife. Robert had hell to pay.

"What friggin idiocy is this?" I said without saying hello or giving Robert the chance to unroll his drawings across the mahogany conference table in our mahogany-paneled conference room.

"Just a minute, please. Give me a chance to explain," he responded. Out came the drawings. If nothing more, they explained Robert's rumpled look, slightly more rumpled than usual. He'd been working on these drawings last night after dinner. Probably all night, judging by the quantity. There were computer drawings underneath, hard lines etched on white paper. On top of these were the soft pastel markings that showed trees, people, kids playing in the yard, tiny little semi-abstract figures, a car—a Porsche—in a driveway and there on top of the flat roofs were people and plants and even a dog.

"You see," Robert said, "the computer is good for showing the big picture. That's what we wanted to get across last night. How this project fit into the universe, how it fit into the Darling family history, how it was structured, relationships, the flow of space, its architectural sensuality. But the computer can't show the human side very well, the people, the vegetation, and the life forces that occur when the architecture is occupied. I thought showing these drawings last night would be just too much, too intimate for such a formal gathering." If Robert was trying to make me believe he had these drawing ready last evening, the pastel smudges on the side of his hand betrayed him.

"But, my dear Robert . . . this is not Poundberry. This has nothing to do with Poundberry. It has nothing to do with the Darling history. It only has to do with your friggin' modern architecture, and I'm sorry, but covering it up with some plants, people, and dogs and their excrement just isn't going to convince me or anyone else that these are homes. Town homes. Village homes. We are trying to create a community here. Communities don't have flat roofs. Shopping malls, industrial estates, apartment buildings, and military complexes have flat roofs. Not even Taco Bells have flat roofs. Nobody is going to buy into this as a community. Who would want to live here? Not me, not my friends, not anybody I know. Do you know anyone who would want to live here besides you and a few of your architect friends? Come on, tell me who? Our market research, the American Home Builders Association, get me? *Home*builders! *Better Homes and Gardens*, the *Architectural Digest*, they are all telling home consumers, the buying public, the real people who are going to live in these residences, not the gnomes you've drawn on top of your computer drawings, no, the real people, the real people, that they want pitched roofs. They want dormers; they want chimneys. They don't want to sit on top of their roof. What nonsense that is. This isn't Paris or New York. People don't have to sit on top of their roofs to get a glimpse of the sun or the moon. I know urban, an urban feel. You've got Darling Mews confused with Paris rather than the Cotswolds. There is a difference between an urban village and an urban slum. Now put some frigging roofs on those plans, give me some fireplaces, and give me some windows rather than glass walls. Give me some brick and wood and stone, and I'll give you people who would like to buy your vision. I like your plans. I like the street layout. I like the 'mews' idea, but in words your cybernaut friend might use, your architecture sucks."

Robert hadn't got past drawing one, an aerial perspective taken from the computerized fly-through we'd been subjected to the night before that showed most of the project as seen by a bird about to shit on the whole thing. He took on that stupefied look again. It was as though I had been talking to him in some damn foreign language and he was trying to come up with a response. *No comprende, no habla Española,* no whatever.

The reality seemed to be that my relationship with Robert was about to come to an end. I wasn't so concerned about that as I was about the relationship between our sons. They had put us together in good faith. They were a part of the deal. And here were these crusty old guys who couldn't agree on some frigging architectural details about to blow the whole project, the whole deal.

"Look, I said, "I like everything about what you've designed except when it comes out of the ground. There we have a problem. You're great with plans, but I think you read the wrong magazines. When we talk about architectural history, you and I are talking about two different histories. Now I have a proposition for you. Let's call your contribution complete. I mean your architectural services. You're finished. I don't mean finished like finished. I mean let's say you've completed your part of the contract. Let me get another architect to put architecture on your plans. We won't change a single thing on your plans. Just let me get someone else, someone who reads *Architectural Digest* and *House Beautiful* to add the architecture. Okay? The project will still read Robert A. Michael and Associates, Architects. You'll get all the credit for the plan; don't worry. The plans are the important thing. It's your plan. I love your plans."

AN EYE FOR THE NEW

The Director

It was remarkable that the firm of Robert A. Michael and Associates, Architects, unknown to the New York culturati, came close to being awarded the commission to design an addition for one of New York's most highly regarded cultural institutions despite the fact the firm seemingly had no New York ties.

Then again, architecture commissions, especially high profile ones, are not dependent upon an architect's locale as they once were. The practice of architecture has become international. Not in the way Johnson and Hitchcock had imagined. The pure international style didn't last long, except in the realm of corporate office building. But look at the distribution of major museum commissions around the world over the last half century: the Pompidou in Paris by Piano (Italy) and Rogers (Great Britain), the National Gallery in London, Venturi Scott Brown Associates (USA), the Sekler Gallery, Cambridge USA, Sterling (Great Britain), the Museum of Modern Art, New York, Taniguchi (Japan), the Art Institute of Chicago and Menil Foundation, Houston, Piano again (Italy), the Guggenheim Bilbao Spain, Gehry (USA). The list goes on and on and continues to grow. It is the "practice" of architecture that has become international, not a style. Selecting an architect for a museum has become as significant as the acquisition of a rarified piece of art.

You look at the list of architects above and match them to a museum and you wonder why. Why this architect for this job? The answer is most often "the trustees." Museum boards represent an elite demographic, each trustee most often coming from a different walk of life. Their one shared attribute is that they have money and influence, preferably lots of money and lots of influence. They are on the museum board because they know what to do with money, they know how to raise money, they know how to spend money, and they know something about art. Sometimes they have art that is worth a lot of money and the prestige that comes with it. They also like power and influence.

To begin my story let me say that after a protracted search, the museum trustees hired me as director making it clear that my job was to bring the curatorial level of the museum and the collection itself up to a higher level and I was to manage the construction of a new wing on land the trustees had acquired, with some stealth, adjacent to the existing museum. To my credit, I might add, I had recently completed the building of a new museum of art at a major university. I had also become known as someone who had an eye for "new" art, especially video art. My age—thirty-six—helped, I was told, though I was concerned that the board of trustees, average age seventy-two, might think I was someone they could push around. My letters of reference, at least one that was shared with me, said, "When push comes to shove, Alex knows how to both push and shove." Push and shove did come about. The problem? The trustees, as they always do, control the line that determines who wins the match of push and shove. The game is always rigged in their favor.

I didn't appreciate this fact when I accepted the position. New York! Who in their right mind would not jump at the opportunity to take a museum job in New York, as director no less, with the promise of contributing to the construction of a high-profile addition? My role was to be the intellectual and spiritual leader, and the trustees were to do the hard work of foraging for money. I just had to set the stage. Money gives to money, they say. The trustees had given significant amounts to other people's causes. Now it was their turn to make "the ask," their turn to raise seventy million dollars. They themselves would prime the pump. The president of the trustees started the priming with a gift of ten million dollars, and others followed suit. They raised among themselves twenty-five million dollars before they took to the streets with tin cups in hand.

You should know that I am now the former director of the museum because of a stir created by the architect Robert A. Michael. No, I wasn't fired, though my lawyers say I would have come out of this battle of push and shove well ahead if I had allowed myself to be fired. I resigned. Robert became my friend, and while he behaved badly, a fact I don't think he still fully understands, he had an artistic integrity I admired. When he was defrocked, what was I to do? I still have a life to live and I have to live with myself and friends, family, and professional colleagues. This was not just an issue of power politics. This was about integrity. I had to stand by Robert. There was no choice in my mind. I became a hero to some who revere anyone brave or foolish enough to stand by their principles. The trustees became the villains; Robert became the victim. It was a play in three acts. When the final curtain fell, only the villains were left standing.

Let's go back to the beginning. As the trustees began discussion of the addition and it became certain that they could acquire the property they would need, I suggested searching for an architect through an invited competition. This was a way of drawing attention to the project, giving it some valuable PR and visibility in New York, the city with attention deficit disorder. At the same time it was a way of establishing a dialogue with the trustees. The architect's schemes would play the catalyst for discussions about everything from function to aesthetics. I was delighted when my proposal met with the unanimous consent of the trustees. A developer on the board offered fifty thousand dollars to fund the competition, ten thousand dollars each for five architects to be selected by the board from a list of twenty to be presented by me.

This is where Medea came in. She knew Robert, and I knew her slightly. She had covered some of our exhibits and had conducted an interview with me for public television. We had lunch after the taping. I liked her. She was a quick take. Her son was a photographer, she noted during lunch, and she had a portfolio of some of his work with her. Pretty good. Reminded me of Aaron Siskind. She also showed me a monograph of the work of an architect. It happened to be Robert's monograph just published by the Princeton Architectural Press. I glanced at it. She urged me to take it along and give it a closer look. She had done her homework and knew that we were about to engage in the competition, working toward a long list of twenty architects.

"Maybe Michael is someone you should consider," she said as she handed me the monograph. Sardonically, she added, "He's from the Midwest, and that makes him almost as exotic as someone from say, Zurich. Midwesterners even have accents." I smiled and obliged her wish, admiring her carefully constructed charm. She seemed to know we would be conducting an international search.

The list of twenty was circulated surreptitiously. I started with about fifty architects, and my staff pulled together articles that showed their work. The staff took a straw vote and cut the list to thirty and gathered additional publications for those. We turned the museum boardroom into a library and encouraged board members to view the material that we had assembled. I wanted to make this process as democratic and open as possible.

My conversation with Medea had totally escaped me. Robert's monograph sat next to my bed and was quickly buried by the art books and catalogues that constituted my nocturnal readings. In fact, as I recall, I was so enthralled by her son's photographs that those images became my preoccupation. I asked one of my staff to find some books on Siskind. I was right to make the comparison.

Leaking the list of twenty before we made it official was a way of testing the street-smart cognizanti. New York is a village. Gossip can move faster through the streets than by social media. A rumor uttered at the bar of the Four Seasons soon becomes fact. Medea heard of the list and was incensed that Robert wasn't on it. She thought she had sealed his selection when she passed his monograph on to me. I believe she thought I owed her a favor because of the flattering words she had been writing about us. She chewed me out for not being "aware" of Robert's talent, his geographical location notwithstanding. And she insisted on sending me a review of the monograph.

The review was from an English architectural critic who praised Robert for his oeuvre and suggested that his work bridged two conflicting tendencies in contemporary architecture: that which values a building because it is true to its mission and that which supports an architecture that is originally conceived, well crafted, and contributes to the discourse on architecture.

I was astounded. This was exactly the discussion my staff was having as we began the process of sorting through architects for the list: should an architect's work fit a particular context and program or should it speak to architecture as an autonomous discipline? It was the polarizing argument of the museum as a white box or as an object in its own right; a building that was responsible to its mission as a cultural institution or a building that like the objects it displayed was a finely crafted object of the highest order and originality.

When it came time for the trustees to meet and to endorse the list my staff and I had assembled, there was some unease among the members. Ten of the names were the usual list of suspects. They would appear on anybody's list of signature architects. The other ten represented trustee favorites, as it were. But there was one among the twenty who had become somewhat suspect. It was rumored that she was going to be commissioned to do another major museum. If she had that job, it would surely overshadow our own. We would look like we were camp followers or trailing dogs or whatever. It was moved that we take her off the list. This left us with nineteen and an embarrassment since it was already public that we would have a list of twenty

Lucky for Robert. I told the board something along the lines of, "Well, this gives me the opportunity to introduce you to someone I think we overlooked in our selection process. His name is Robert

Michael. He's just published a monograph that has received wide international recognition for the caliber of his work." A slight exaggeration, but I passed around a copy of the article by the British critic that Medea had sent me along with Robert's monograph. It elicited some ahas, some umms, and a few didn't even open the book. The meeting was getting on. Some of the trustees were about to leave. A motion was made to include Robert A. Michael so we could round out the list to twenty. Done.

A letter went out to the twenty the same day. They were requested to send a portfolio of their work, their qualifications, and a letter stating what particular qualities they might bring to the project. A brag sheet. Robert called me shortly thereafter, asking if he was seriously under consideration. "Yes," I said. "How had we heard about his work?" I told him the story of having lunch with Medea and her passing along his monograph and how impressed I was by the review in the British journal. He didn't seem surprised.

Everyone via this letter was informed of the conditions of the competition. Of the twenty, five would be selected for the competition. A news release announcing the competition was published but not the names of the twenty architects. However, the architectural establishment knew in no time. The museum had to come up with another fifty thousand dollars to administer the competition. A neutral referee was selected to oversee the process and to make sure the competition abided by its own rules. They also helped to write the brief, the program statement, and gathered all the background material the finalists would need: aerial photos, zoning and other pertinent codes, photos of the surrounding area, plans and sections of the existent museum, the museum's most recent catalog, etc.

I drafted a statement concerning the museum's objectives in conceiving this addition for discussion with the trustees. Most of the board didn't want to be bothered. One famously said in front of the others, "I don't know what I am looking for, but I'll know it when I see it." Remindful of the US senator, or was it a Supreme Court justice, who so claimed when asked to define pornography.

We went into this as a jury of twelve trustees and myself. Thirteen votes. At one moment I felt like I shouldn't vote so I could maintain some neutrality, and at other moments I felt I should have more votes than anybody else because I was the one that was going to have to live day and night with this decision. In the meantime the trustees said, "Let's not worry about the voting and hope that we will be able to reach a unanimous consensus in our support of a winner." Amen.

A month passed before we had all the submissions. Some sent us books of their work. Others were presented in the standard portfolio format. Two didn't submit letters, and one sent us a proposal for the building. It was a little insulting to have some of the more renowned firms send us material in a rather dismissive way, as though we were getting the leftovers from other submissions they had made. Oh, and one said they no longer participated in competitions and another, a Japanese architect, sent us a letter saying that he was flattered to be considered but felt that he could not, if he were to receive the contract, control the quality of construction in a city with a very different building culture. He withdrew. The list of twenty was reduced to fifteen with two withdrawals, one disqualification, and two who had not sent submissions and were taken out of consideration. The fifteen left made a mixed bag of contenders.

Before I go on, let me tell you a little about the trustees, because they are a key part of this whole story. Twelve very independent minds. I won't name names, but here is the cast of characters in no particular order:

A. An octogenarian architect with an immense art collection that every museum wanted to get their hands on, an avowed tastemaker
B. Another octogenarian—this one a grand dame whose family helped to establish this institution and endowed it with both works of art and cash
C. An art historian, critic, and collector who also saw himself as a tastemaker
D. A bank president who pioneered the idea of the "corporate collection" and whose collection it was said constituted an unbelievably large part of the bank's assets
E. A former gallery owner who had galleries in five cities, three domestic and two abroad, who quit the gallery business after her third divorce when she became fabulously wealthy
F. A socialite and habitual volunteer who made it a habit of wearing all the right clothes at all the right times in all the right places

G. Her designer with an address book chock-full of social and entertainment celebrities
H. A real estate tycoon who discovered that you could make incredible profits buying and selling real estate you could hang on your wall or put on a pedestal in your entry foyer
I. The owner of a livery service who was reported to have warehouses full of art that the museum hoped to acquire as a gift someday
J. Another real estate tycoon who owned an undisclosed but not insubstantial part of midtown Manhattan and who made the land deal for the museum's addition
K. A lawyer who had a reputation for representing artists, artists' estates, foundations, and whatever and whoever mattered in the art world
L. A famous actress with a degree in art history who was married to a famous director who together assembled a fabulous collection of avant-garde art

All of them were knowledgeable, to a degree, about the art world. They all loved the museum. They all certainly loved being on the board, though they would much prefer the social status that the position brought them over the sometimes difficult matter of providing oversight to the museum's operation. A board meeting inevitably grew into a contest to see who had the most financial acumen or their pulse on the latest artist's auction price or a sense of what "others" were doing or whatever. To say that this group was competitive would be a gross underestimate. But as some might say, "That's New York for ya."

Of all the portfolios and letters of interest we received it was Robert's that captured my attention. Quite surprisingly, I would say, his was the most graphically sophisticated. It read like a book and wasn't so much a portfolio of his work as it was a portfolio of ideas and teases that incorporated images of his work juxtaposed with images from the museum's collection and passages from poems and literature that tied all this together to narrate a deep understanding of the museum, its purpose, and future. When I finished looking at it, I thought this is something we should have commissioned.

Robert's portfolio began with a quote from Ad Reinhart's "Twelve Rules for a New Academy": "The present is the future of the past, and the past of the future." It was accompanied by a picture of one of Ad Reinhart's black abstract paintings, a cornerstone of our collection, with a facing photograph of Robert's own house taken at night with the lights of the city and stars in the sky creating their own pointillist composition. The portfolio/book went on in this manner, combining the images from the collection and images of Robert's work. One kept flipping through the pages until the images seemed to merge and the association of Robert's work with the objects and artists in the museum collection was firmly embedded in your mind. Its acoustic equivalent would be listening to a composition that was so hypnotic you could not get it out of your head even after the sound was gone. Robert created an afterimage that merged the world of the museum with his own world.

While Robert's entry seemed to deconstruct the museum's collection and put it back together to fit his own aims, other entrants seemed hardly to recognize the museum's collection at all. Most ironic were those that showed museums they had previously designed but apparently had them photographed before the installation of any of the art works. What were they trying to prove? If it was that they didn't care for art, they succeeded.

I thought that Robert would be a certainty when it came to the selection process that would now narrow the group of fifteen down to five for the competition. I was wrong. Wanting to bring whatever influence I could muster on the selection of the five contestants, I approached each of the trustees separately before the decisive board meeting to get a sense of what they were thinking. These conversations would range from "What do you think?" to "What does so and so think?" to "Oh I know for certain who they will be" to "I'm a busy man and have not had time to look" to "Do you think this is the best way to select an architect?" I remained enthralled by Robert's presentation and couldn't understand why others didn't seem to be. *Damn*, I said to myself, *there is only one presentation that gives a shit about who we are as a museum.*

The board meetings were usually a lunch affair, catered by EAT, the highly regarded Upper East Side establishment, which created an incentive for board members to arrive on time. The meeting would start at 1:00 p.m. and end with cocktails around 3:00 p.m. The board preferred having a few long meetings rather than lots of short ones. These were not social occasions, but we tried to make them pleasant. It was often difficult before 5:00 p.m. to keep people away from the bar set up next to the boardroom even though we would serve wine with lunch. The lubrication always seemed to help in the early part of the meeting, but some of the older members would start to nod off around 3:00 p.m. if the meeting should reach a lull. They would revive themselves about 4:00 p.m. and head for the bar to quench their thirst, as they would put it. We were lucky to get three quarters of the trustees together at any one time; business was the most common excuse for absenteeism, though vacations played their role as well. But the day of the finalist selection we had full attendance.

Several trustees gathered in our wood-paneled, plush carpeted and bedraped boardroom well before noon to look at the submissions, some for the first time and others to refresh their memories. There were four trustees who hadn't looked at the portfolios and letters yet. I was infuriated at their cavalier attitude after all the work that had gone into assembling this material for their review. I put Robert's portfolio on top of the pile to make sure it got the attention I thought it deserved.

The minutes of the meeting would show that there was a half-hour discussion as to how we would proceed. I suggested that we discuss each candidate, but that was rejected as taking too long. Someone else suggested that each member have the opportunity to present a candidate of their choosing, but that was thought to take too long as well. It was finally decided to take a straw poll and in a secret ballot write the names of the five candidates each would like to see considered. In that way we would have a rank of preferences. A few of the less well prepared asked if they could have a few minutes to look at the submissions again, having a difficult time remembering five names. I was asked to have the staff provide a list of the candidates, which we did. All this took about an hour.

The balloting revealed five clear winners. Robert was not among them. I was discouraged. There were no surprises here. The top vote getter was the architect of the month who had just come off a string of critically acclaimed museum and gallery projects, each looking similar to the last. You might say he was from the white box school of museum design. The second was a New York favorite, his choice heavily influenced by the octogenarians. The candidate was an octogenarian himself. The third and fourth were both foreigners, one from Europe who was known for his high tech and always over budget extravaganzas.

I was surprised that he was even interested in this project except for the opportunity to build in New York City. The other was Japanese and not concerned with the problems of building in the United States. He had already done so. The fifth was a corporate firm best known for their office structures and without a museum in their portfolio, but they felt they owned New York, and obviously so did some of the trustees.

Robert tied with three others for sixth place. Before I could say a word, the president of the trustees asked if someone would move to approve the top five vote getters as the slate for the competition. The motion was rapidly made and seconded. He was about to say "all in favor" when I interrupted. "Wait, we need time for discussion. This was going to be a straw vote, remember, so we would have a basis for discussion. I really think we should be discussing at least the top eight candidates." There was a clear demarcation between the highest-ranked eight and the next tier. I suggested that we begin our discussion with these candidates and decide if we wanted to discuss any others.

There were pained looks from some of the trustees who were ready to move to the cocktail hour and the self-congratulatory toasts that would launch the competition. A discussion? Their minds were already made up or had been made up for them. There had already been a lot of back room political maneuvering to get to this point.

"Yes," said F, to my surprise. "I can't say I am all that happy with the top five, and I would love to meet this fellow Robert A. Michael. His book is smashing. I am going to ask him for a copy. It should be published. It is apparent that he knows the museum and our collection better than anyone else being considered. Just look at his presentation and the way he has shown us images of his own architecture and the way his design ideas relate to our own collection. He not only made a presentation of his accomplishments; he made a statement."

"Maybe I missed something," said K. "Let me see that Michael guy's submission again." I passed him the book. "Hey, look at this reference to Ad Reinhardt," K said. "His estate would love this."

It was decided to take a quick break to allow for going to the potty (as one trustee preferred to call our breaks). It also allowed time for getting a drink and looking at the submissions of the now eight finalists, once again, and to allow time for hushed kibitzing. The boardroom could have benefited from more corners to accommodate these conversations. The trustees could be divided along many different lines. I would often describe them, jokingly and in confidence of course, as a board that could be divided horizontally, vertically, and diagonally. But, as I've said, they were all very independent and ready to avoid an identification with any peer group. In actuality there were several natural divisions. There were the dealmakers: the real estate, banker, developer, and lawyer types who tended to see art as a commodity. They enjoyed playing in this commodities market as much as the stock market because the products were tangible, something you could display and have the bragging rights to. Then there were the tastemakers, those who loved art for its aesthetic merit but also enjoyed the opportunity to show the world how much they knew and to set the standards of taste for their peers and the public at large. There were also divisions by age and connections (family ties) and associations, old money and new, etc. There were also divisions along the lines of who owned what art pieces themselves, who was influencing who and what, and who had what to give to the museum and speculation about wills and works on loan, etc. These were much more fluid associations that tended to emerge and merge and change when discussion of acquisition policy arose and planned exhibits, etc., became a part of the board's agenda. Now these eight architects had become a part of the board's portfolio, and the discussion would be which to keep and which to discard. Whose stock would rise depending on how the board felt it would be judged by this selection and what this selection would say to the world of art and architecture?

I saw F busy talking during the break, not to the usual cadre of tastemakers that she was a part of but to the dealmakers. First I and then H and K. Then she came to talk with me. "You know, Alex, I had the most divine lunch the other day with this woman named Medea Galas. She writes about architecture and art and was raving that we were considering Robert A. Michael for the competition. She said he was really someone we should consider seriously. I said no one had ever heard of him, but she said it's not because he isn't talented, and she gave me a copy of a monologue of his work that had recently been published. The pictures were very beautiful. I almost forgot this conversation, Alex, but then I looked at Michael's submission, and it is beautiful. Isn't it? Don't you think he should be one of the five? I mean, really, the others are so predictable. It would be nice to have one stranger in that crowd. After all, we have the reputation for discovering artists; shouldn't we have a reputation for finding architects as well? I've been talking with some of the others, and I think they agree that a new face wouldn't be all that bad." So Medea had had lunch with others. I wondered whom else on the board she had touched. Clearly enough to get Robert considered among the eight, or was it simply the merit of his submission that people were now reconsidering? A buzz seemed to be going around the room as his book was being handed from one trustee to another. It was time to get back together.

D, president of the board, called the meeting back to order. J said, "Well, I think we've all had a little time to consider our first vote. If there isn't any discussion I would like to move ahead and take another straw vote to see what the outcome is now that we have narrowed the list to eight and have had some time for additional consideration. We'll see who the top five are this time, and then we can have a discussion. Any objections?" D said before anyone had time to consider J's proposal. There was a general nodding around the conference table as my assistant handed out slips of paper that included the names of the eight finalists. F looked my way and gave me a little wink. We hadn't talked about whether I favored Robert being in the competition, but she knew nonetheless.

My assistant counted the ballots. The order had changed. Robert A. Michael had replaced the corporate architect on the list of the top five vote getters. As soon as the tabulation was announced J usurped the role of D, the president, and said, "Is there any discussion?" D, one of the most conservative members of the board, said, "Well, I don't know. We are replacing one of New York's most-established firms with this firm from the Midwest, and we hardly have anything to go on except this book that he sent which proves that he was at the museum and saw our collection, but is he a good architect really?"

F spoke up. "Really!" she said. "Didn't you see how he displayed his own architecture in juxtaposition to the works in our collection? He's not only showing us that he knows the collection; he's showing us how his design could complement our collection. I thought that was pretty amazing."

"I think it's amazing too," said E. "It doesn't make any difference where he's from. Most of New York's most fabulous artists, architects, and celebrities are from somewhere else. He's just not fortunate enough to have a New York address, poor dear. I'm sure if he wins the commission he'll open a New York office, and then we can call him one of our own."

MISUSED ALLEGORY

The Trustees

Robert's competition entry was as elegant as the submission he had created for the board's initial consideration. This time, instead of a book, he submitted a video. He met all the other qualification prescribed by the competition administrators: plans, section, perspectives, a model, and all that. But in Robert's entry his model of the museum and his proposal for an addition doubled as a container for a videodisc. Lift up the hinged roof and there was a compartment, exquisitely crafted, that held the disc. Robert knew that I had made expanding photography and video art in the museum's collection a priority and that that was one of the goals driving the creation of the Blaustein Wing.

The addition now had a name. The Blaustein Wing was named after the president of the board, who had given the largest and pump-priming gift to begin the museum's fund-raising. All five finalists, because of the addition's limited site, used a fairly obvious parti. The original museum was built in the shape of a U with the interior of the U developed as a sculpture garden that had become largely disused and neglected by the museum. Each of the five contenders chose to fill in the U in various and predictable ways—a winter garden, an atrium, a site for a monumental piece of sculpture to be commissioned, a sculptural circulation system of elevators, escalators, and stairs, and a void, simply a void. The void was Robert's idea.

When Robert made his presentation to the board, a collective sigh was heard when it appeared that Robert was going to tear the top off his wooden model. There were rumblings from some of the trustees, of course. What was the big idea of doing something beyond what had been called for? Of course that was the big idea. Despite some protest, the lights were dimmed and a portion of the room's back wall slid away, revealing the projectors that museum staff used to do their work. One of my staff inserted Robert's disc.

The video was a twin to the book that Robert had submitted with his qualifications that put him into this final round. But now the art of the museum played off the architecture proposed by Robert. The museum and the addition were shown seamlessly through a video animation. And the magic was in the images that took on a reality before your very eyes. Or so it seemed. The camera quickly became you, the audience, moving through what began as a line drawing of Robert's proposal; white lines against a black background, reminiscent of an early Frank Stella or a Joseph Albers playing with three-dimensional illusions. The comparison was not lost on some of the trustees. The image stopped long enough to gradually transform itself from a sketch outline to a fully rendered space. The flat planes of the sketch became articulated surfaces, floor, ceiling, and walls. Just as seamlessly art appeared, our art, a painting, a piece of sculpture, and then, then people would appear first as ghosts and then as animate objects. The camera moved to a glass stair in what Robert described as the void that separated the old from the new and descended to the video section; visible signage noted that. We entered a foyer, and people stood back to let us enter as though we were a privileged few attending the opening of a new video installation. The image before us faded from light to darkness, and there before us was a video from our own collection, one of Bill Viola's first.

I recall that moment when the trustees sat there stunned. I knew that Robert had it in the bag. How could anyone take the time to look at the other submissions after seeing this? There was a visceral quality to Robert's presentation. We had all just been inside the museum, and now we had to step back outside it to this boardroom so that we could commission it so we could get back inside it . . . for real. The trustees were visibly excited. Not only had Robert given them an exciting presentation; he had given them a fund-raising tool "extraordinaire." But the exhilaration did not last forever.

Is beauty in the object or in the eye of the beholder? Is it the rationalists or the empiricists who are correct? That was the question I posed for myself in my dissertation—my incomplete dissertation. Perhaps I should go back to it. But what have I learned in my role as museum director? I have learned that the object, the object maker, and the viewing public constitute a dialectic whole; that is, the art, the artist, and the audience together comprise any artistic enterprise. Good enough for a thesis topic?

Even before the board decided to ask Robert to sign a contract, he was asked to make a copy of the video for each of the trustees and several more for use by the museum staff. It was a very short time after the video was distributed that I received a call from L. She wanted to see me. She and her director husband had watched the video together, he for the first time. Something in the video had caught his well-trained director's eye, and they played the tape back for themselves several times. There on one of Robert's virtual walls hung a picture by the photographer Robert Mapplethorpe titled *Fist Fuck*. They were very familiar with Mapplethorpe's oeuvre and had in fact managed to obtain this particular photograph as a gift to the museum after the gallery that owned it had been threatened with a fire bomb upon displaying this and other Mapplethorpe works from his S&M series, which had already caused a sensation in Cincinnati and Washington, DC. The museum's acquisition was not heralded for obvious reasons, but the museum had accepted the gift and treated it as an important part of their photography collection even though it was never given public display on one of its walls. I was very happy this had all happened before my time, and the museum's handling of this gift never caused a stir. Now Robert had purloined the controversial photo that showed a fist and arm of a man inserted in the anus of another man. Somehow Robert had retrieved the photo from the archives and hung it on a wall of the museum's new virtual annex. L insisted that I watch the video with her. After seeing it, I wondered why no one had caught it before, but I presume that because we were all so enthralled with the medium we didn't see the massage. (Excuse me, Marshall McLuhan.)

Now there were multiple copies of the video floating around. Which trustee would be the next to see this little trick Robert had played on us? And, what if it occurred during an audience with a group of potential donors? All could not be as blind as we were when Robert showed us the video. There was nothing to do but call a special meeting of the trustees.

On such short notice it was impossible to assemble all the board members, but the staff was able to get a quorum. No mention was made of the purpose of the meeting. I let L tell her story. Shocked looks appeared on the faces of the nine members present. Some of the newer members of the board were not familiar with the fact the museum had a copy of *Fist Fuck* nor with its controversial history. L elaborated on how this photo and others by Mapplethorpe had inspired then-senator Jesse Helms to try to shut down and defund the National Endowment for the Arts, the government institution that was so important in helping the museum finance its special exhibitions program. Even though the NEA's contribution was always modest, it served as a form of endorsement in attracting other funding. Since the Helms affair, however, the NEA had been forced to change its objectives, and there was little chance that their funds might be used to support anything that appeared to be controversial—i.e., to be pornographic. Nonetheless, the museum continued to find programs the NEA might support. There was still a palpable fear among museums that the government might play an even more serious role in censoring art.

To break the silence, one of the trustees asked whether *Fist Fuck* was actually on public display. I assured them that it was not. "But anyone seeing this video might think it is," he retorted. It was late on a Friday afternoon when this meeting was held. It was decided that the matter was too important not to have a discussion by the full board, and I was ordered to arrange such a meeting as soon as possible. None of this was to be leaked to the press. Even though the bar was now open, no one wanted to linger, and everyone scurried off to a weekend where they could put their minds to other things.

My first instinct was to call Medea. I suspected that she contributed to both of Robert's presentations, including the video. Her answering service said she would not be taking calls until Monday. Robert and Medea did not have to break into the museum's archive to capture an image of Mapplethorpe's *Fist Fuck*. A little research could find this image here and there. It had garnered much press. In some circles it acquired celebrity status.

I reached Medea, or rather her answering service did, before the weekend was over. Through her service I had asked to get together with her for breakfast on Monday, a ploy to suggest that I had a serious matter to discuss with her, and it did prompt her answering service to contact her.

We met at a midtown hotel at 8:00 a.m., an ungodly hour for types like her and myself. I got to the point quickly. Members of the board were disturbed by having seen Mapplethorpe's *Fist Fuck* photo on the virtual walls of Robert's proposal. Why had they, implicating Medea in this adventure, done this? Medea looked me in the eye and said without blinking, "That image was the inspiration for Robert's proposal." A sucker punch if there ever was one. I hadn't seen that coming. It wasn't just a controversial picture displayed inappropriately in an architectural presentation; it was a picture that had inspired an architectural concept. Who would have guessed? What was bad had become very bad. How could this be explained to the trustees? The reality was that it couldn't. The analogy of the *Fist Fuck* and Robert's insertion of his proposed addition into the existing museum was apparent once the idea was planted. Once suggested, it was an image impossible to dismiss, just as Robert's video presented an image that made his proposal and the museum's collection inseparable.

I suspected that something was afoot when several trustees didn't return my calls and then the president called me to say that he had set a meeting of the trustees at his club and demanded my presence. I asked what the agenda was. He said, "My building, idiot, and don't bring Mr. Michael."

D, finally assuming some leadership as president again, had arranged for a private room at his club. When I arrived, I found the trustees already assembled, and it was apparent that the meeting had been going on for some time. D was pointing at drawings pinned on the wall. I craned to see the authors. It was the corporate architectural firm that was kicked off the competition list to make room for Robert. D was obviously quite excited in making the presentation. He saw me enter the back of the room. "Come in, come in, Alex," he exclaimed. "I think we have the problem solved."

"And what problem might that be?" I exclaimed, wanting to hear his own explanation for this meeting and his actions and what I saw on the easels behind him.

"Alex, you know. Don't act naïve. We can't go ahead with Michael's project. Not after having learned what inspired the concept for his design."

How did this get out? I thought it was only Medea and Robert who knew the backstory. Medea?

D went on, "If this got out, his metaphor or whatever you call it, we would be the laughingstock of New York—of the art world itself. I showed my wife the video and she was disgusted and appalled that we'd even consider such a scheme. 'My God,' she said. 'You'll only have queers attending the museum if you let this get out.'" D had evidently forgotten there were queers on the board.

"I've consulted with our lawyers," D announced, "and they have assured me that we have no contractual obligation with Robert A. Michael and Associates, Architects. As you can see, I already have someone else who is interested in the project."

"But," I tried to respond. "But—" and D cut me off.

"Come on, Alex. This is more important than all of us. You know that. I've already consulted with the board, and this is the direction they've chosen to go." And as a drowning man sees his life pass before his eyes, so did mine.

Of course word did get out. There were all kinds of stories floating around the city. Fortunately none had come to the attention of the press. With twelve trustees there would be twelve stories, and time would only embellish them. The project died, stillborn. The corporate architect wised up and considered the bad publicity it would suffer entering into a contract with the museum that broke the rules of the competition for this commission they did not need. They withdrew, an embarrassment to D, the president, but of no great concern to the remaining trustees. The trustees had lost their nerve. They didn't want to pursue the expansion, the bad publicity it might bring, and the accusations and the explanations, and yes, it was the publicity, wasn't it? They cursed Robert. Of course they did want the publicity, which was why they were on the board, or one reason. It enhanced their identity, but not this publicity. This was not identity-enhancing publicity. They had seen what had happened in Cincinnati and the takedown of the Corcoran in DC, and God forbid did not want to be a part of what might become a rekindled saga centered on Robert Mapplethorpe. Ironically, Mapplethorpe's exquisite photography, after this episode in his career, focused primarily on still life's that were claimed to be erotic by a continuing army of detractors. His death brought greater acceptance of his work.

D, as president and the board's spokesman, decided on his own to take the matter to the press before rumors had a chance to metastasize. He avoided a press conference that would surely have attracted a TV crew. D. instead issued a news release that said the trustee's had concluded the second stage of the selection of an architect for its new addition but instead of proceeding at this point had prudently decided it needed to focus on strengthening the museums endowment before moving ahead with the addition. D. meanwhile called Robert to tell him he would personally make sure his career was destroyed if he leaked any of the backstory. He also called me to say the same thing. I had no intention of saying anything to anybody.

Some board members, after they had heard D. might have threatened my job, called to assure me I had their support. But I didn't intend to keep my job. It would be easy to get back in the marketplace. Directorships turned over frequently. After all, it was the board who aborted the project, and they had promised me that I could lead this venture. It was easy enough to tell the art world I was ready for a "real" opportunity. But it would be difficult to find one to match this. This was New York City, after all.

Medea heard about D's news release and called me wondering why I hadn't called her to tell her the bad news. What had happened? I said I had nothing to add to the news release. She knew better. She insisted on meeting with me. Lunch? There was no way I was going to discuss this over lunch in a New York eatery. In Nova Scotia maybe. Part of having lunch in New York is listening to the conversations from the tables around you while you are at the same time babbling about your own project. It is a high art form. New York is full of professional gossips.

Instead we agreed to meet in Central Park behind the Met. It was the first time I recognized Medea's beauty. Perhaps it was seeing her at a distance. I was the first to arrive and found a bench that was free. She didn't see me. Her walk was the silky smooth glide one saw on fashion runways. Her arms hung loosely by her side with a voguish purse slung over one shoulder. Her head turned side to side, obviously looking for me. Her features were tanned, but it could also have been an olive complexion, the kind women from the Mediterranean have, that burnished bronze look, fashioned by time and good breeding as well as a gentle sun.

She saw me and with a few long strides sat beside me on the bench, not at the other end, but as close as she possibly could looking me straight in the eyes. "So why the fuck-up?" she said as only a woman well seasoned in New York's street culture could.

I recounted the entire story, parts of which she already knew: L's director husband who had spotted *Fist Fuck* in the video, attention given to it by the entire board, fear of the publicity and repercussions it might bring, etc., the decision to abandon the project entirely, my decision to look for other employment and . . .

As I was saying all this, I could see she had become self-absorbed. "Wait," she said. "I wondered how Robert became familiar with *Fist Fuck*. Now I get it. It was that damn Naut and his LGBT friends. It was Naut who was familiar with that photo and must have told Robert about it and compared his proposal to the photo, and Robert took the bait and said it was the photo that had inspired him when all the time the two were never connected. It was Naut who must have hung *Fist Fuck* on the virtual wall. Did Robert even catch this?" Medea noted how she and Robert were concerned with looking at the architecture and hadn't paid much attention to the art that Naut chose to insert in the video.

I didn't know this guy Naut, someone in Robert's office I presumed. Medea seemed anxious to pin the blame on someone else and take the pressure off Robert. "If the project were to be reestablished could Robert be considered again?" She didn't seem to understand the seriousness of the affront the board felt now closely associated with the two Roberts. K had offered to discretely handle the sale of the Mapplethorpe if the museum wished to de-accession it. *Fist Fuck* had surely gained in value. E had once hung out at the Ramrod, the gay bar in Greenwich Village, and told K. he still had acquaintances from there who would surely be interested in such a purchase. The trustees did eventually authorize the sale of *Fist Fuck* after I departed.

DENIAL, ANGER, BARGAINING, DEPRESSION, ACCEPTANCE

Charlie and Robert

The following interview, made for public television, was recorded a few weeks before Robert's disappearance. The interview has been edited for the purposes of this account.

Charlie:

Our guest is Robert A. Michael, an architect who recently had a monograph published of his work of the last thirty years and who was selected for the celebrated museum project that has been a source of much gossip here in New York. A *New York Times* reviewer points to his minimalist houses in the sixties and his present proposal for an entire community using new-urbanist principles as capturing all the contradictions that have faced his profession over the latter part of this century. I would like to start this interview more tactfully, but this is the question everyone has for you: why?

Robert:

Why? Where would you like me to start?

Charlie:

No, you begin. Why do you think people are asking you the question "Why?"?

Robert:

Well it could be why was the museum project abandoned? That's a question I have been pledged not to answer. Why did I become an architect? Why did I have such a difficult time with my clients? Why did I crave publicity? Why, why, why. There are so many whys!

Charlie:

Let's begin with why you had such a difficult time with your clients.

Robert:

Well, I didn't really mean that.

Charlie:
But you said it.

Robert:
Well, I meant my clients and I often have differences of opinion. Especially over aesthetic matters.

Charlie:
Explain.

Robert:
Clients should know when they hire Robert A. Michael and Associates, Architects that they are employing someone who steadfastly adheres to modern aesthetic principles. That is what brings me to the attention of most of my clients in the first place. But once we are into the project, they soon forget why they hired me, and I have to keep reminding them. And that sometimes creates friction.

Charlie:
You've been accused of being bombastic by some of your clients, even those who were very satisfied with your work.

Robert:
Perhaps that is the artist in me coming out. I don't like to be criticized. I am a professional. I have professional opinions when it comes to my work. And I expect people to respect my opinion and not quibble over this or that just because they don't like it.

Charlie:
But architecture is a public art. It is unlike a painting or sculpture that can find seclusion in a gallery or museum or over someone's couch. Architecture is out there for people to bump into. In its own way it is a commissioned piece of public art. It's unavoidable. Doesn't that matter?

Robert:

Of course it matters. That's why I am an architect. I want people to see and experience my work. But I don't think popular taste or lack of it should dictate what gets designed and built. We have too much of that. That is why the world is so ugly. Tastes change or evolve. Modernism showed us the way. It hasn't been allowed to evolve in the way it should. Tastemakers. I hate them. Taste making has become an industry. No wonder the twentieth century was never allowed to develop an aesthetic of its own.

Charlie:

I recently met with one of the trustees of the museum whose design you won through a competition. She said a key factor in awarding you the design was the monograph that had been produced of your work. In the preface to the monograph a British architectural critic and architect calls your work "a distinguised oeuvre by this architect just coming into his own." You are fifty-something?

Robert:

Fifty-six.

Charlie:

I know, fifty-six, and this critic says you are just coming into your own. You've been practicing for thirty years, and it says in the monograph, to repeat, that you are just coming into your own when many professionals your age are beginning to think about retirement. Do you plan to work until you are ninety or a hundred like Philip . . . Philip Johnson?

Robert:

It takes a long time to become an architect, to become known, to get good commissions, to be recognized so you get better commissions.

Charlie:

Is that why your work is featured in this very handsome monograph? Is that why you are on this program?

Robert:

Yes, of course. You have to have your work published, and you have to have work to be published. You have to become recognizable. Building a building, any kind of building, takes years, and unless you have a very large firm you can just do so many buildings a year. So . . . yes it takes thirty years before you have anything really substantial to publish. People won't find you just because they looked in the Yellow Pages for an architect.

Charlie:

The editor for the monograph is Medea Galas, a journalist known in New York for her coverage of the art world. And I understand that you are married to her. Isn't this a little disingenuous to have your wife as your editor? Isn't this a lot like Eero Saarinen the highly regarded modernist architect and mid-westerner from Detroit marrying Aline Bernstein, also a New York journalist who became his help mate, his publiscist?

Robert:

Well, I never thought to make the comparison. I met Medea as she was covering the PA architecture awards.

Charlie:

And Aline was covering Eero's design of the GM Tech Center when they met.

Robert:

Can we change the subject?

Charlie:

You've mentioned Ayn Rand as an influence. I presume you were referring to her book *The Fountainhead*. You said you once admired Rand. I presume by that statement you no longer do.

Robert:

I was young when I discovered Howard Roark . . . not sure what I wanted to do or be. I read comic books and my favorites were Superman, Captain America, and other superheroes. I wanted to become a cartoonist. When I read *The Fountainhead* I thought Roark was like these superheroes. Thanks to Rand I actually thought architects had superhuman powers unlike artists.

Charlie:
And?

Robert:
Well, I gave up on Rand when I became aware of her political agenda. I don't believe in politics or religion and philosophy has really screwed up a lot of architects. I stay away from that stuff. Rand betrayed a lot of young men wanting to be architects. Me included. I'm still pissed at her and her abhorrent philosophy, which has nothing to do with reality, nothing to do with being an architect.

Charlie:
So you have had a successful architectural practice. You've won awards, been recognized, won competitions, and had a monograph published of your work, and still it seems as though you are struggling with your career as an architect.

Robert:
Struggling, I guess. We still turn down commissions that we don't like or don't suit us. It's not because we don't need the work. We live by our principles.

Charlie:
What are those principles? What architectural camp do you fall into?

Robert:
I've tried to avoid falling into a camp as you call it. There is no one prevalent architectural philosophy any longer. For a time there were three camps in the United States. The Whites, the Grays and Silvers. One might call them the rationalists, the

pragmatists and the empiricists but those labels don't easily apply anymore. In the Midwest, where I mostly practice, architects tend to be pragmatists. It's all about the bottom line for most of our clients. If you get the bottom line right aesthetics will take care of itself, or so most of my clients think. Sometime ago there seemed to be more Whites or rationalists on the east coast and Silvers or empiricists on the west coast but those categories no longer really apply. All seems to be chaotic today.

Charlie:
So which of those worlds do you inhabit or did you inhabit?

Robert:
I'm from the Midwest. Born in the Midwest. Practice in the Midwest. Didn't I just answer your question?

Charlie:
I know, but in what you describe as today's chaotic world, and by that I presume you mean the many aesthetic movements going on at any one time, isn't it possible to be a rationalist, an empiricist, and a pragmatist at the same time?

Robert:
You could say I am a blend of all three, rationalism, pragmatism and empiricism. My architectural education was on the East Coast. Corbu, the French/Swiss genius and his rationalist theories certainly influenced me. Mies van der Rohe and minimalism, his pragmatism, has been a strong influence on my work. I design with the site—nature or context—as a starting point, and I do want my work to enhance people's sensual pleasures. But if I told my clients what I've just told you, they would have no idea what I was talking about. I have my own theory of architecture—what I try to achieve in my work. Do you want to hear it?

Charlie:
Yes, of course.

Robert:

In one word—ambiguity. I believe there are three stages in the life of a building. The first stage is during construction. People stop and stare at a building being constructed. It captures their imagination. They have to participate in imagining what the building will become. The second stage is when the building becomes inhabited; it simply takes its place with other inhabited buildings. In a way buildings just disappear unless they become part of an intellectual discourse generated by the world of architectural critics. The third stage, when the building becomes a ruin, once again engages people's curiosity. They stop and stare and wonder what the building was. Ruins are a major contributor to the world's tourism industry. My goal is to create in the finished building an ambiguity similar to what stages one and three possess. Ambiguity. That to me is a characteristic of the twentieth century. Science has eliminated certainty. Today science provokes more questions than it answers. With all the tools at an architect's disposal, shouldn't we be producing buildings that ask their observers to participate in the experience of experiencing? And like abstract painting, that participation is often achieved by what is absent, what is not there to be observed, the ethereal.

Charlie:

Don't you sometimes wish you had chosen to be an artist rather than an architect?

Robert:

Hasn't everyone dreamt of escaping his or her past? I imagine the world to be full of people who think about vanishing without a trace to begin life anew, under a new name, with a new personality, perhaps even a new occupation. I still dream of shaping my own destiny even if it might not be as an architect. You have reminded me I wanted to be an artist even before I chose to become an architect.

Charlie:

Thank you, Robert.

EPILOGUE

Robert remains disappeared.

Wife no. 1 moved to San Francisco and is married to Emily. They have two adopted children.

Daughter Amy completed her degree in architecture from UC Berkeley and is working as a project architect for Skidmore, Owings & Merrill.

Andrew (Robert's former son-in-law) left his law practice to develop an e-commerce start-up. Capitalized at two hundred million dollars, his venture is still looking to make a profit.

The observer has his own thriving design/build firm.

Ms. Jones was successfully treated for breast cancer. She does volunteer work for many arts-related groups.

Medea lives in New York with Naut. Both have been in and out of treatment for their drug addiction.

Conrad is attending the Culinary Institute of New York and has given up photography. He has told his mother that he is HIV positive.

Koko was asked to be in a photo shoot for *Ebony*. She married a white guy from South Africa who is also an architect. They moved to Paris where they opened their own practice on the strength of her work with Versace.

Reverend Ike saw fund-raising for the addition to the AME church go better than expected, and the congregation decided to use their extra funds to expand the sanctuary.

Cybernaut worked for a time designing computer games (also see Medea above).

Son Chip has joined Al and Mitch Darling in the development of Darling Mews.

Alex the museum director is teaching contemporary art history at NYU and doing independent curatorial consulting.

Fist Fuck, the photo, was quietly sold to an undisclosed buyer for an undisclosed price.